THE PERKS OF MEDDLING

THE SIDEKICK'S SURVIVAL GUIDE MYSTERIES, BOOK 2

CHRISTY BARRITT

River Heights

COMPLETE BOOK LIST

#10 Glitch and Famous (coming soon)

Raven Remington
Relentless 1
Relentless 2 (coming soon)

Holly Anna Paladin Mysteries:
#1 Random Acts of Murder
#2 Random Acts of Deceit
#2.5 Random Acts of Scrooge
#3 Random Acts of Malice
#4 Random Acts of Greed
#5 Random Acts of Fraud
#6 Random Acts of Outrage
#7 Random Acts of Iniquity

Lantern Beach Mysteries
#1 Hidden Currents
#2 Flood Watch
#3 Storm Surge
#4 Dangerous Waters
#5 Perilous Riptide
#6 Deadly Undertow

Lantern Beach Romantic Suspense
Tides of Deception
Shadow of Intrigue

The Art of Eavesdropping

The Perks of Meddling

The Exercise of Interfering (coming soon)

The Practice of Prying (coming soon)

Carolina Moon Series

Home Before Dark

Gone By Dark

Wait Until Dark

Light the Dark

Taken By Dark

Suburban Sleuth Mysteries:

Death of the Couch Potato's Wife

Fog Lake Suspense:

Edge of Peril

Margin of Error

Brink of Danger

Line of Duty

Cape Thomas Series:

Dubiosity

Disillusioned

Distorted

Standalone Romantic Mystery:

The Good Girl

Suspense:
Imperfect
The Wrecking

Sweet Christmas Novella:
Home to Chestnut Grove

Standalone Romantic-Suspense:
Keeping Guard
The Last Target
Race Against Time
Ricochet
Key Witness
Lifeline
High-Stakes Holiday Reunion
Desperate Measures
Hidden Agenda
Mountain Hideaway
Dark Harbor
Shadow of Suspicion
The Baby Assignment
The Cradle Conspiracy
Trained to Defend

Nonfiction:

Characters in the Kitchen

Changed: True Stories of Finding God through Christian Music (out of print)

The Novel in Me: The Beginner's Guide to Writing and Publishing a Novel (out of print)

CHAPTER ONE

IF THERE WAS one thing my mama had taught me, it was to mind my own business.

My dad, on the other hand, had told me that meddling, when done correctly, could change the world.

The contradicting advice wasn't lost on me. In fact, for most of my life, I'd felt torn between being the person I was raised to be and the person I knew was buried down deep inside. Nature versus nurture collided and caused an earthquake inside me.

I'd like to say I was picking up the pieces, but the truth was that I was actually still dealing with the aftershocks.

As the thoughts lingered in my mind, I slammed my car door and walked toward Driscoll and Associates.

Would the new investigative part of myself rise to the

surface? Or should I be content organizing files while crunching numbers with the speed of a math addict?

I still wasn't sure.

It was Monday morning, and I stepped into the office building just in time to see a woman slip into Oscar Driscoll's office. Oscar, my boss, reminded me of a Mayan king who sat on a throne atop his temple supervising his peons with disdain. The woman appeared to be several years younger than I was, probably in her late teens or early twenties.

I knew about Oscar's reputation for going through assistants like some people went through toilet paper. Was he interviewing someone to replace me?

I'd only worked here a week, and I'd already been fired once.

But I wouldn't put it past him.

I glanced at Velma, the receptionist, and asked, "Who's that?"

She shrugged and continued to study her bright red fingernails. "I don't know. She just wandered in here from off the street. Looked like she'd been crying. I'm actually surprised that Oscar agreed to meet with her considering she didn't have an appointment."

So this wasn't an interview.

This woman was a potential client.

"Donut?" Velma shoved a box toward me.

I shook my head. "No, thank you."

I'd learned to never eat anything Velma brought in. She

was a dumpster diver, and most of the food wasn't safe—no matter how appealing it might sometimes look. I heard she once even took some leftover food off someone else's table while dining at a restaurant.

She went beyond cheapskate and into off-her-rocker territory.

Before I could walk to my desk, I heard a cry come from behind Oscar's closed door. Whatever reason that woman had come in, it wasn't good. She was obviously struggling.

Velma and I exchanged another look.

I took a sharp left turn and crept closer to Oscar's door. I put my ear against the wood. This job had taught me a thing or two about eavesdropping, but I bet Oscar never thought I'd use those skills on him. However, I wasn't above that. Not right now, at least.

I tried hard to listen to what was going on, but I could only make out a few words. *Sister is missing. No one will help.*

My heart pounded into my ribcage.

I desperately wanted to be in that room and hear what was going on. I wanted to know if there was some way we *could* help. Investigating was getting into my blood, for better or worse.

Footsteps sounded, and I barely had a chance to step away before the door flew open.

The woman hurried past me, wiping her tears as she rushed toward the exit. I glanced at Oscar, waiting for his explanation. He simply shrugged as he sat at his desk.

"What can I say?" he muttered. "She can't afford us."

Something rose in me when I heard his words. That should never be an excuse for not helping someone, right?

But Oscar would disagree. He'd already moved on. I could hear his TV blaring in the background.

"As soon as Michael gets here, I need to see the both of you in my office," Oscar said. "Got it?"

Michael Straley was my coworker and the one who was showing me the ropes on the job.

"Got it," I said before turning to Velma. "Listen, I forgot something in my car. I'll be right back."

Without wasting any more time, I hurried outside. I spotted the woman who'd left the office and hurried toward her. "Wait!"

She glanced over her shoulder, as if she hadn't expected me to call out to her. I quickly observed her honey-blonde hair, slim build, and big eyes.

I jogged until I reached her and then paused. "I work for Oscar. He said you couldn't afford us. Is that right?"

She wiped her red eyes using the sleeve of her pale pink shirt. "I figured I couldn't, but I thought coming here was worth a shot. I always hear about people doing *pro bono* work. It just never seems to happen like that for me."

"I'm not sure if I can help or not, but, if you don't mind me asking, what's going on?"

Moisture filled her eyes again. "It's my sister. She's missing, and nobody is taking me seriously. No one believes something criminal may have happened."

I needed to back up a few steps and get some more basic information out of the way. "What's your name?"

"Rebecca Morrison." She glanced up at me, and her face twitched as if she was barely holding herself together.

"Rebecca, I'm Elliot Ransom. Tell me, how old is your sister?"

"Twenty-four."

"And when was the last time you spoke to her?"

"It's been three weeks, but she left home about eighteen months ago."

I took mental notes of everything she told me. "Is it weird for you not to hear from her for that long?"

The woman shrugged. "Not really. It's part of the reason no one is taking me seriously . . . including the police. She has a tendency to disappear and then resurface."

I turned away from the glaring sun so I could see Rebecca better. "Why do you think this time is different?"

"My gut tells me that it is. I can hardly sleep at night because I'm so worried about her." She sniffled before a desperate cry escaped. She turned away so I couldn't see the agony on her face.

It was too late. I'd seen it. And I could relate.

I touched her arm, compassion pounding inside me. "What's her name?"

"Trina. Trina Morrison." She thrust something into my hand.

I looked down and saw a picture of a woman with dark-brown hair, a slim build, and symmetrical features. "She's pretty."

"I know. That's Trina. That's always been part of her problem, I suppose. She's pretty, and she's not afraid to use it to her advantage."

I looked down at the picture again, and my heart pounded in my ears as a decision stretched before me. I was new at this. I barely knew what I was doing. I was hardly qualified.

But I was passionate, and I cared. Could those qualities make up for my weaknesses?

I could take the case, though I wouldn't be an ace. But I could do this as a perk each day after work.

That wasn't great, but you should try to put a rhyme together quickly. It was harder than it might seem.

I had a slight fixation with rhyming, especially when I got nervous. It was a coping mechanism my dad had taught me.

"Listen, I know that Oscar said he won't take this case," I told her. "But I might be able to help you on the side."

Hope flooded her gaze before quickly disappearing. "I don't have the money—"

"I'm not doing it for the money. I'm doing it because we all need someone to help us out sometimes."

The breath left my lungs as the woman pulled me into a

sudden—and tight—hug. "Thank you. Thank you so much. I don't even know what else to say."

"Don't thank me yet," I told her. "Not until you see if I can find some answers or not. How about if we meet tonight at The Board Room. Do you know where that is?"

She pulled away, her eyes full of hope. "Down in the harbor area?"

"That's right. Can you be there at six?"

"I'll do my best. But I have to be at work at seven so we won't have much time."

"We'll make sure it works. I'll see you then, okay?"

"Okay. Thank you. There's one other thing," she added.

I paused. "What's that?"

Her voice cracked as she said, "I think the Beltway Killer is responsible."

THE BELTWAY KILLER? A shiver raced through me.

He'd already killed four young women in the DC area, each time leaving their bodies near the circle of interstates surrounding our nation's capital. As far as I knew, the police had no leads. But everyone in the area had been living with a new sense of fear, waiting for the killer to strike again.

I certainly hoped Rebecca's sister hadn't been taken by the man. There would be no happy ending if she had.

As I stood there a moment watching her retreating figure,

my phone buzzed. I pulled it from my pocket and glanced at my screen, certain it would be my sister, Ruth, texting me another silly selfie. It was her latest obsession. That and something called TikTok.

Instead, I blanched at the words I read there.

Stay away or else.

Stay away or else?

Tension threaded up my spine, and I glanced around me.

Was someone watching me? Had they seen me talking to Rebecca and wanted to warn me not to get involved?

Or could this go much deeper?

Could this somehow have ties to my father, whom I'd recently found out had been a spy in my home country of Yerba in South America? I suspected his death wasn't due to a heart attack, as it had originally seemed.

I suspected he'd been murdered.

The thought caused a mix of grief and tension to thread my muscles. Maybe my soul.

I didn't see anything suspicious around me.

Just buildings with their cheerful façades, their pleasant plant boxes filled with colorful flowers, their tidy white shutters.

Everything in this town looked clean and neat.

A little too clean and neat, if you asked me.

It was like the town had to work extra hard to make sure

it looked spotless, like a trash can that was flawless on the outside but full of rot in the interior. People only did that if they wanted to cover up something.

I saw nothing unusual around me. A woman walking her dog—a snobby looking poodle that knew it was pretty. A man in a suit hurrying by with his phone to his ear. A jogger who barely glanced around before crossing the street.

But no watching eyes.

So who was this text from?

I didn't know. The number was blocked.

But I needed to get into work right now.

I turned to go back when I collided with someone.

Hands reached for me.

And I knew I was in trouble.

CHAPTER TWO

"ELLIOT?"

I blinked as the figure came into view. "Michael?"

"I didn't mean to scare you." He studied my face, not bothering to hide his curiosity. "What are you doing out here? You look pale."

I waved my hand in the air, trying to shake the feeling that I was being watched—and to forget about the threat I'd just received. "It's nothing."

I hadn't told Michael about my dad or my recent discovery about Dad's career. I definitely hadn't mentioned that my father might have been murdered or that someone had been watching me the past week or so.

Michael was around my age—late twenties—with a stocky, muscular build. He had numerous tattoos, dark hair that was always covered with a backward hat, and a boyish vibe.

Today, he wore a T-shirt that proclaimed, "The Earth Is Flat."

I was pretty sure he was just trying to mess with people's minds when he wore stuff like that.

But I wasn't certain.

And that was probably exactly what he wanted.

He glanced around me, and a knot formed between his eyes. "What's up?"

"Long story," I told him.

A healthy dose of skepticism stained his observant eyes. "I bet."

A case of nerves rushed over me, but I shoved them aside. Instead, I needed to deflect this conversation. My dad had taught me that rule in the journal he'd left me.

I glanced at the time on my imaginary watch. "You're running late."

He frowned as we began to walk toward the office. "Sorry. Chloe forgot one of her books, so I had to drop it off at school."

"You're a good dad."

He shrugged and pulled the door open. "I don't always feel that way. It's hard trying to be both mom and dad to a seven-year-old. But I have managed to master how to braid hair."

I flashed a smile at the thought of Michael, with his thick

fingers, trying to manage such a delicate task. "I think you're doing better than you give yourself credit for."

He offered a tense smile, one that showed he didn't quite believe me. "Thanks for the pep talk. But I think we should probably get inside. Oscar's already texted me three times, and he used the angry emoji this last time."

"That's because you broke the number one rule. Never be late. Oscar's the only one allowed to do that." Velma had gone over all those rules with me when I'd first been hired. Other rules included never wearing a red dress around him.

He was messed up, I was pretty sure.

Michael rolled his eyes. "Yeah, I know that all too well."

Something about Michael seemed off his game today. He was usually so laid-back and fun-loving. But today there was a new heaviness to him.

Granted, I'd only known him eight days. Sometimes, it already felt like a year, and other times like we'd just met. Either way, I was glad our paths had crossed.

We walked inside together, and Oscar's booming voice accosted us from across the room. "You two! Get in here! Now!"

Michael and I glanced at each other before walking into the office.

Oscar was large—both physically and in a larger-than-life kind of way. His nose was bulbous, his head nearly bald, and his mustache noteworthy.

We sat in the chairs across from Oscar and waited for

him to begin either telling us what we needed to do or telling us what we had done wrong. Most likely, he'd be telling us both.

There once was a girl who couldn't do anything right, and her new boss seemed to be all bark and no bite. But she knew down inside her there was a fighter, and she had to remember to try to shine brighter.

After we'd solved the last big investigation for him, a case involving professional golfer Flash Slivinski, Oscar had been praised on TV for being such a great detective. Little did anyone know that he hadn't actually done any of the work.

I liked to mentally call myself the imposter's apprentice since Oscar was officially supposed to be teaching me the trade. Instead, he watched soap operas and took all the credit for other people's hard work. However, he paid nearly twice what I'd been making at the health insurance agency, and I found satisfaction in the work.

So I stayed.

"I've got a job for you two," Oscar started, popping some pistachios in his mouth. "It's an insurance claim."

"Those are the worst." Michael ran a hand over his face, already looking more exhausted than he had earlier.

"They're not exciting, but we need to do it. I want the two of you to work together. You can keep each other alert that way."

I hadn't done an insurance claim yet, but I had heard Michael mention several times that they weren't fun.

People wanted to make surveillance seem interesting when, in fact, it was torturous. Kind of like having to go to the bathroom in the middle of the jungle when there were no facilities for at least sixty miles.

Michael leaned back, reminding me of a college boy listening to an assignment from an old, crusty professor. "What is it this time?"

Oscar rattled off the details of the case. It seemed pretty cut-and-dried to me. A man named Nolan Burke had filed a workers' comp claim. He said he threw his back out and could no longer work in the tool factory that employed him. He handed Michael a photo so we could identify him if we saw him.

His boss wanted to be sure he was telling the truth. It was up to Michael and me to prove that this guy was a liar and a fraud. We just needed to catch him in the act.

Oscar dismissed us with the flick of his hand, almost like a ruler dismissing his minions. That Mayan king analogy came back to mind. At least the man wasn't wearing a loin cloth.

I paused in the doorway before leaving. "Quick question."

Oscar looked up at me, something close to annoyance. "What is it, señorita?"

"Why didn't you take that girl's case?"

"The girl that just left here?" His face scrunched with annoyed confusion. "I don't do cases pro bono."

"Why not?" His blanket statement seemed heartless.

"Because that's not how you stay in business."

"Don't you ever just see someone you want to help, despite the fact they may not have money?"

He didn't even blink. "This is my business, and I decide which cases we take. Not only did that woman not have any money, but she didn't have a case. From what she told me, her sister has a history of disappearing. There's no need for us to waste our time on that."

But I remembered Rebecca's tears. They'd been real. And I intended on helping her if I could.

Just like I hoped someone might find mercy on me and help me fund my own sister's life-changing lung transplant surgery.

AN HOUR LATER, Michael and I were parked near Nolan Burke's house. We were in Michael's old minivan, a vehicle that had seen better days. That made it perfect for this job—no one should notice it.

However, I had to resist the urge to wipe down his dashboard, to neatly collect his trash into one place, and to track down every stray french fry.

Michael was many things, but not neat.

Burke lived in a small bungalow, not much different from the one I lived in with my mother and sister. His car was in the driveway, so Michael and I assumed he was at home, but we'd yet to see the man.

We'd picked up some coffee on the way here, and I had a feeling it was going to be a long workday for me. I reminded myself not to drink too quickly or I might have to go to the bathroom.

First world problems. I was beginning to understand them more and more all the time.

"So, how was your weekend, Elliot?" Michael turned toward me, studying my face for a moment as his hand brushed the subtle prickle on his chin. "Did you go out with Jono yet?"

Was it just me or did his voice take on a mocking tone when he said Jono's name?

Jono was a well-known rich guy and playboy here in town. He liked dating a lot of different women, apparently. I wasn't really interested in him, but I thought he might have information on my father's death.

In order to confirm that, I needed to get to know him better.

"Funny that you ask," I finally said. "We're actually going out tomorrow night."

"Going out on a date on a Tuesday? Times have changed since I was dating."

I studied Michael, trying to interpret his statement. There were still some Americanisms that I had trouble picking up on. "But we're the same age almost."

"I haven't dated in a while, though."

I crossed my arms and continued to study him. The man was good-looking in an edgy, athletic kind of way, so I found his statement hard to believe. "And why is that?"

He shrugged and stared out the window. "It's hard to find someone who will let me be a good dad to Chloe and be a good boyfriend. The balance is tougher than you would think."

I squinted in thought, trying to put myself in his shoes. "Why?"

"I guess when you're dating someone, they want to feel like they're the center of your world. But Chloe is the center of my world and . . . it's really hard to find someone who's cool with that."

Chloe's mom had abandoned her daughter when the girl was two months old. I didn't know all the details. Michael hadn't shared yet. But I was curious about their story.

"I'm sure you'll find someone, and everything will fall into place." I meant the words.

In the short time that I'd known Michael, he seemed like a good guy. Loyal. Hardworking. Fun-loving. What was there not to like? When the right woman wandered into his life, everything would fit, would work out.

"Yeah, well, that said, my dating life is not my favorite thing to talk about." He put his car seat back and stretched, almost as if he wanted to take a nap—or avoid the rest of this conversation. "We're going to be here for a while."

I reached into my bag and plucked a book out. "I always carry a backup novel just in case."

"Just in case what?"

"Just in case I get bored or I want to practice social avoidance."

He chuckled. "Social avoidance? I like that."

"If you only knew." I'd also found the bathroom a great place to escape when I'd had too much people time and just needed a moment alone.

I glanced out the window at the house, which was still as dormant as a river in dry season.

"So we just sit here and wait to see if Nolan Burke comes out?" I asked. "And if he does come out, we see if he does anything to indicate he's not really injured, right?"

"You've got it. And if he goes anywhere, we follow him. This is the part of PI work that I can't stand."

I frowned. "I have to admit it doesn't sound like much fun."

It reminded me of that time my dad had taken me into the jungle to watch the dorado catfish, which migrated from the Andes up to the mouth of the Amazon. It happened only once every couple of years, and he wanted me to see it.

I'd desperately fought boredom as we'd waited for four days to see the fish. The event itself had only lasted an hour.

That's what this felt like.

Michael ran a hand over his face. "It's not fun."

A moment of quiet fell. The two of us were just getting to

know each other, but Michael was an easy guy to talk to. That said, sitting here for hours on end might put that theory to a test.

"So, what were you doing standing on the sidewalk earlier?" Michael asked. "Don't tell me nothing."

"Fine," I said. "If you must know, I was talking to a woman named Rebecca."

"And who is Rebecca?"

"Rebecca is someone who was hoping that Oscar would take on some pro bono work for her. He said no. Does that surprise you?"

Michael let out a little snort. "Surprise me? No, not at all. I figured you would have figured that out about Oscar by now. He's not a pro bono type of guy."

"It doesn't surprise me. I'm just holding out hope that Oscar will redeem himself, that there's a good person buried down deep inside."

Michael pressed his lips together, as if he was biting his tongue. Instead, he said, "So, something about this woman must have caught your attention."

I remembered my conversation with her. "Her sister's missing. I guess her sister has a bit of a troubled past, but no one seems to care that she's gone. No one except Rebecca."

"How did you end up talking to her?"

"I followed her when I saw her leave." I shrugged, unsure what kind of story he'd expected.

Realization washed over Michael's face, and he let out a

long, low chuckle. "Oh no, Elliot. I know what you're think-ing, and that's a bad idea. Get it out of your head."

I glanced at him. He could already read me that easily, couldn't he? "Get what out of my head?"

"You're thinking that you can take on the case on the side."

Maybe he *could* read me that easily. "And if I *was* thinking that, would it really be all that bad?"

"Oscar doesn't like it when we do things on our own like that. Besides, you probably signed some type of noncompete agreement in that paperwork you filled out when you first started saying that you can't do investigative work on the side."

"It's not like I would be doing it for money. I would be doing it out of the goodness of my heart. Why would that possibly be an issue?"

Michael sat up and turned to me, all the humor disap-pearing from his gaze. "You've only been doing this for a week, Elliot. I'm not saying that you haven't done a good job or that you don't have some natural talent. But I think it's a little premature for you to be taking on investigations on the side, with or without that noncompete agreement that you signed. That's a true fact."

Facts by their very nature were true, making his state-ment redundant. Every time he said those words, I cringed and wanted to correct him. But he was a button pusher, and I had a feeling that was the only reason he always said that. Kind of like his shirts.

I turned fully toward him, ready to plead my case. "But you should have seen her, Michael. She was really upset. Someone needs to help her, and the police told her she doesn't have a case. Do you know how hard it is to feel invisible?"

"Then maybe she will find another PI somewhere who will help her." Compassion—and unyielding conviction—rang through his voice. He wasn't going to change his mind about this.

"But what if she doesn't?" An innate vulnerability stained my words, and I looked away. I hadn't intended to share that.

Michael's eyes softened. "I can imagine it's hard. Let's hope her sister comes back. If the police don't want to take this on, maybe there's a reason for it. Maybe this woman disappeared because she wanted to, not because something went wrong."

I licked my lips, understanding his argument but not ready to accept it. "But if it was your sister . . . wouldn't you want someone to help you?"

"Of course, I would, but . . ."

I stared at him. "What?"

He shrugged and ran a hand over his face. "I don't know, Elliot . . ."

"I'm just saying, if I were in her shoes, I'd want someone

to step in and do something for me." I crossed my arms. My mama always said I meant business when I did that.

His gaze softened. "And I'm not saying that's a bad thing. That's part of what makes you good at what we're doing. You really care about people. I'm just saying that you have to make good choices. To use one of your jungle analogies, I'd hope you run away from the charging jaguar instead of running toward him."

"Exactly. Good choices. That's exactly what I'm making." I nodded, feeling a touch of satisfaction stretch through me. He did understand.

Should I mention her theory that the Beltway Killer was behind it? I wasn't sure.

But before I could figure it out, the front door to Burke's house opened, and a man stepped out. He was tall and lanky, with light-brown hair and an unshaven face. As he ambled forward, his hand went to his back, as if he was in pain.

The man looked around before climbing into his car and cranking the engine.

In one fluid motion, Michael raised his seat back to the upright position and gripped the steering wheel. "Let's see where our friend is going."

CHAPTER THREE

MICHAEL HAD BEEN correct when he said doing surveillance work was awful. It had definitely felt very similar to the migrating dorado catfish experience.

We'd followed Burke as he drove through a fast food drive-thru, then as he'd taken a walk, and, finally, as he'd stopped to visit a friend.

But the one thing he hadn't done? Anything that might prove his workers' comp claim was a sham.

Michael and I got back to the office at five, knowing we'd need to continue this job tomorrow. I could hardly contain my excitement.

And, yes, that was sarcastic.

My mama constantly told me that sarcasm wasn't "becoming," as she liked to call it. But I had to admit that I kind of liked it. The American way was rubbing off on me, but I wasn't sure that was a good thing.

Either way, I had just enough time to make it down to The Board Room to meet Rebecca and find out more about her sister. Despite the conversation that I'd had with Michael about the case earlier, I was still equal parts excited and convicted.

Once I got an idea in my head, it was hard to change my mind. And right now, I definitely had an idea in my head. I was like a stubborn mule on the way to a well. It was a Yerbian expression, and even I wasn't 100 percent sure what it meant.

I wanted to know what had happened to Rebecca's sister, Trina. One way or another, I was going to find out.

"See you tomorrow, Elliot," Michael called as I walked toward the door.

I looked back at him and saw the glance he gave me. It was almost as if he realized exactly what I was doing. But there was no way of him knowing that.

Right? I wasn't *that* transparent.

It didn't matter. I got into my beat-up Buick and headed down to The Board Room.

The restaurant was my new favorite place to go if I ever had any extra money to spend, which I rarely had. Okay, in truth, I'd only been here twice. But I'd loved it both times.

The place was not only a casual restaurant that featured charcuterie boards of all types, but there was also any type of board game that you might want to play there. The atmosphere invited people to stay, to linger, to connect. Fast food restaurants? They beckoned people to hurry. Expensive restaurants? They called for people to spend money and brag about it with food pictures on social media.

This place just allowed people to gather. To be.

In my estimation, at least.

The eatery was located in Storm River, but it was in a less affluent part of town. Don't get me wrong—in only a few steps you could be in the upscale retail area that politicians and people from old money liked to frequent. But this part of town, with its little harbor and smelly seafood restaurants, was a part of the original infrastructure of the area. At least, that was what I had been told.

I climbed from my car and started across the parking lot. As I did, that feeling hit me again.

The feeling of being watched.

I remembered the text I'd received. *Stay away or else.*

I glanced around, wondering if the person who'd sent it had followed me here.

I still wasn't sure what exactly the sender wanted me to back off on. Rebecca's case? My dad's?

Both of them were potentially dangerous in their own ways.

Just like earlier, I saw no one watching me.

But I couldn't shake the feeling that trouble had followed me.

The question was: Would I be able to shake it this time?

I WENT inside The Board Room and said hello to the hostess before glancing around. I didn't see Rebecca there yet, so I grabbed a table by the window and glanced at the time on my phone.

Rebecca was five minutes late.

As I waited, I ordered a small cheese, cracker, and pepperoni board. It came with some grapes, olives, and walnuts as well. The food would give me something to munch on until I got home, and it was one of the cheapest options on the menu.

I tried to watch my spending because of my sister. She needed to have a double lung transplant, and my mom and I were saving every penny possible to make that happen. Ruth was number twenty-four on the transplant list, and, when it was time for the surgery to happen, we needed to have the money in place.

I wanted to say that the thought didn't make me nervous, but it did. Though I trusted God to provide, the human side of me had trouble letting go. But I was working on it.

Since my dad died two months ago, we'd all pitched in to make ends meet.

My family had only moved here a few months ago from

South America. Political unrest finally came to a boiling point, and my family had gotten out of Yerba right in time.

I glanced at the time on my phone again.

Rebecca was ten minutes late now. I'd give her a few more minutes before I called it quits. In the meantime, I grabbed some dominoes and began building a tower, making sure all the ends were square. Order was an obsession of mine.

Even though doing this off-the-books investigation might get me fired, something about Rebecca and her story grabbed me. Maybe it was because there was a small part of me that wished somebody would step in and help me out.

Don't get me wrong, I liked to make my own way and to do things for myself. But sometimes it felt like the hole I was trying to get out of just kept getting deeper. I felt more like I was burying myself than I was finding the freedom out of the pit.

I nibbled on a cracker and a piece of cheese and glanced at the door one more time. Maybe I would start eating my food and, if Rebecca wasn't here by the time it was gone, then I would leave.

Just as I was on my third cracker, I felt a shadow standing over me and looked up.

Rebecca stood there, panting, with her hair disheveled.

I stood, alarm racing through me. "Is everything okay?"

She nodded. "Yes. Sorry I'm late. I've been having some car problems and . . ."

"I know what that's like," I said. "I ordered this cracker board. You're welcome to have some."

"Thank you. I appreciate it." She picked up a cracker but only nibbled on it.

I leaned closer, getting right to business. I knew we didn't have much time. "I'd love to hear anything else you might have to tell me about your sister, Trina. I know she moved out eighteen months ago and you haven't heard from her for three weeks. But do you have any idea whom I could even speak with to begin to get an idea of what might have happened?"

She pulled a paper from her purse and slid it across the table to me. "As a matter of fact, I typed something up. I listed all the addresses where Trina lived after she moved out. I also included the phone numbers of her ex-boyfriend and her former best friend."

"Former?" I hadn't missed her use of that word.

Rebecca shrugged and rubbed the edge of the cracker with enough force that crumbs rained down on the table. "Trina went through friends like some people go through coffee filters. She isn't the most loyal person in the world. But I know she used to be close with these people. Maybe they know something."

"Have you tried to talk to any of them?" I had to resist the urge to snatch that cracker from her. I hated wasting food. It went back to my humble upbringing, I supposed. Waste not, want not.

"I did try to contact them a couple times, but they blew me off. I'm just Trina's little sister so they didn't take me very seriously." She frowned and rubbed the cracker even more fervently.

Outward motions indicate inner turmoil. My dad had told me that also.

Rebecca was definitely under some strain.

"I see. Do you have any other brothers or sisters?" *Look away from the cracker, Elliot. Look away.*

She shook her head and set the cracker on the table in favor of adding a domino to my tower. It was crooked, but I didn't fix it.

Maybe I would before I left.

"No," Rebecca said. "It was just me and Trina."

"What about your parents?"

Moisture pooled in her eyes. "My dad left when I was little, but my mom is still around. She works all the time or hangs out with her new boyfriend. Honestly, I think she's on the same page as the police. She just assumed that Trina would leave one day, and that's what she thinks happened now."

"Is there any other reason you think something bad has happened, other than just your gut feeling?"

"Trina's just never gone this long without being in touch with me. Sure, she has a tendency to disappear for spurts of time. But she always comes back and checks on me. I'm her little sister, and she likes to know that I'm doing okay. The fact that she hasn't called to see if I'll really be graduating in another month? That raises all kinds of red flags in my mind."

Graduating? I made a mental note of that. "Where do you go to school?"

"Just to a community college. My classes are done by five-ish and then I go work at the local McDonald's to earn some extra money."

I studied her face for a minute and saw the scar near her hairline. "What happened there, if you don't mind me asking?"

Rebecca touched the mark before pulling her hair down over it. "It's nothing."

I knew I'd struck a nerve and shouldn't be nosey, but the woman had me curious.

"It's not important." Rebecca wiped beneath her eyes, almost like she wanted to cry, but then she pulled herself together. "So what do you say? Will you help me?"

I drew in a deep breath, knowing I'd need to answer this question sooner or later. I had to make a choice. "What if I find out what happened to Trina, but it's not what you want to hear? Are you going to be okay with that?"

She hesitated for a minute. "What do you mean?"

I didn't want to ask her how she would feel if the news was bad—if something happened to her sister. Instead, I asked, "What if she's fine and just hasn't been in touch?"

"I'm telling you, she wouldn't do that." Rebecca's gaze

narrowed with stubborn determination and maybe even some loyalty.

I knew better than to push too hard. I needed to respect her boundaries. I'd let whatever evidence I found speak for itself. "You really think the Beltway Killer may have grabbed her?"

"She fits the description of his victims." Rebecca picked up a toothpick and stabbed an olive on the wooden board between us.

A bad feeling swirled in my gut. She was right. The serial killer preyed on pretty women in their twenties who were relatively unattached.

I wasn't quite ready to jump into my first serial killer case yet, so I hoped her assumption wasn't true.

Finally, I nodded. "I'm willing to see what I can find out for you."

Her eyes lit, and she dropped her uneaten olive onto the table. "Would you? I can't tell you how much I would appreciate it if you did."

"Don't get your hopes up. I'm relatively new at this . . ." I felt it was only fair to warn her.

"I can tell that you're cut out for this type of thing. Thank you so much. When do you think I'll hear from you again?" She stared at me, hope filling her eyes.

I had absolutely no idea how to answer. "How about this? If I find out anything, I'll give you a call. Otherwise, how about if we meet again on Wednesday?"

"That's great. Thank you." She reached across the table and gave me a hug.

"It's no problem."

As she stood there, she jotted down her number on a scrap of paper and nibbled on her bottom lip. "You might not want to tell anyone that I'm the one who hired you to find her."

"Why not?" What sense did that make?

"It's just that . . . her friends didn't like me. I was always trying to get Trina to leave them behind. I told her they were bad influences. Some bad blood might be there."

I nodded. "I understand."

"Now, I need to get to work. But thank you. I look forward to talking to you again."

I nodded and told her goodbye.

I'd just promised to help her, I realized. I hoped I hadn't just opened myself up to more trouble than I could handle.

CHAPTER FOUR

I KNEW my mom was working at the drugstore tonight and that my sister was hanging out with one of her friends, so I was in no hurry to get home. I figured there was no time like the present to dig into this case. Besides, working helped me to not focus on other things in my life that were seemingly out of control.

Though I'd never been one to pride myself in staying busy, I did find the behavior was good medicine for not worrying. That's why I decided to pay a visit to Keith Freddie, Trina's ex-boyfriend.

I plugged his address into the GPS on my phone and studied the route for a minute.

Storm River was located anywhere from forty-five minutes to three hours outside Washington, DC, depending on the traffic. I liked to refer to the area as the playground of the rich because this was where they all came on weekends after work.

The nice part about the town was that, as you traveled northwest toward DC, you hit other small towns, which became larger and larger as you got closer to the metropolitan area.

Even though Rebecca said that she was from Storm River, apparently her sister lived closer to DC in a town called Edgerton.

Since I hadn't been in the States that long, I was still learning to navigate this area. But it was springtime, and our clocks had been set back. That meant I had more hours of daylight right now. According to my estimations, I had just enough time to get in and out of the area before things potentially got dicey.

As I headed down the highway, I put in an old CD of one of my favorite singers from back home and sang along as I traveled. I was probably the only twenty-something that still listened to CDs, but I didn't care.

Pablo Stephine was worth it. Just hearing his mellow voice took me back in time.

Finally, thirty minutes later, I pulled into Edgerton. As I traveled deeper into the city portion of the area, I noticed more trash, more graffiti, and more people on the streets.

I knew if Michael was here with me, he'd warn me against doing this. He was partly a mentor and partly a big brother to me.

A slight tremble of worry went through me as I parked on the street and climbed out of my car. I looked at the paper again to confirm the address, and it appeared I was at my destination.

I paced over to the sidewalk and paused in front of the eight-story apartment building that was Trina's last-known address. Two scary-looking men hung out by the door, smoking cigarettes and staring at me.

Another wave of anxiety washed over me as I realized I was going to have to get past them to enter the building.

It was more than these men, though. Something about this area just felt dangerous. Could it be the people loitering on the streets? The graffiti? The way people stared at me as if they knew I didn't belong there?

I wasn't sure.

My dad taught me a lot of things. He taught me to trust my instincts and even to defend myself. But the one thing he hadn't really taught me was street smarts. At least, not in our little Amazonian country. Jungle Smarts had been more practical.

"You can do this, Elliot," I told myself.

We all needed a little pep talk sometimes, even if it came from within ourselves.

Despite that pep talk, my feet did not move from the sidewalk.

"Fancy seeing you here," someone said beside me.

I jumped at the unexpected voice. But, as I looked over, I saw Detective Dylan Hunter staring at me.

The same Detective Dylan Hunter who worked for Storm River Police and looked like Captain America. We'd interacted briefly when I'd worked undercover cleaning the police station as part of my last assignment.

"What are you doing here?" I blurted before I could stop myself.

"I might ask you the same question." His eyes glimmered as he looked at me.

The man had classic good looks and a reserved attitude that made him hard for me to read. His hair looked dark blond sometimes, light brown at others. His eyes were blue and intelligent. His features were . . . well, they were undeniably perfect.

"There's one thing we can both agree on," I finally said. "It's not illegal for me to stand on this sidewalk, right?"

His expression remained stony. "It depends on why you're standing here."

"This isn't exactly your jurisdiction so I'm assuming you're not working a case." Actually, I didn't assume that at all. The man was dressed in a long-sleeved shirt that was rolled to his elbows and some casual jeans.

"No comment," he said. "But I can tell you this is a rough area of town for you to be wandering around by yourself."

I glanced around, keeping my tone light. "Is it? I hadn't noticed."

His jaw shifted, either in annoyance or amusement. Maybe a touch of both. "And that's exactly what I'm afraid of."

I glanced at the building, realizing I needed to get a move on before daylight disappeared. "Rest assured, I don't want to keep you."

Hunter followed my gaze. "You're not planning on going in there by yourself, are you?"

That didn't sound good. "I thought about it."

He pressed his lips together in a frown. "It's not a good idea."

"It's just an apartment building." I swallowed hard, wondering about the truth in my words. "It's not like it's an abandoned factory or a former insane asylum . . . right?"

"It's a place filled with drug runners and prostitution rings. I've seen people go into this place and never come out."

A shiver washed through me, especially when I heard his dead serious tone. "Really?" Was he just making that up to scare me? He might be the type. I wasn't sure.

Hunter nodded, no hint of teasing in his gaze. "Unfortunately, yes."

I nibbled on my lip as I contemplated my next move. Not knowing what else to say, I finally murmured, "I see."

My words seemed noncommittal enough.

The detective continued to study me, and I felt the heat rising up my cheeks. I didn't like it when men had this effect on me. Sergio, my ex-fiancé, had also made me react like this.

I almost felt like I couldn't be myself. I was too overly aware of every word I said and every movement I made.

I didn't want to respond like this—or to think like this—or to act like this. But I was.

"Why don't you tell me what you're really doing here and maybe I can help you?" Hunter's words sounded measured and precise. "Are you working another case for Oscar?"

"I'm actually not here on official business." That was the truth, at least.

"Are you going to tell me why you really are here? Obviously, you're under no obligation." One of his hands casually went into his pocket as he waited. "Maybe I can help."

His stance made it clear that he fully expected me to answer that question.

There once was a girl who was trapped. An escape plan she should have mapped. But now she was stuck in what felt like muck, and she just might have run out of luck.

I shifted, entirely too uncomfortable with this conversation. "Somebody asked me to help them. Off the books," I blurted.

"Do you mind if I ask who?"

I shrugged. "Kind of."

He continued staring at me until I blurted, "Rebecca Morrison."

Realization rolled over his features. "You're looking for her sister."

"That's right. This is the last place she lived. That

Rebecca knows about, at least." I knew I wasn't going to get any information from him, so I kept talking. "She told me the Storm River police won't help her."

"That's not true." He shook his head. "Trina's last known address, as you said, isn't in Storm River. It's not our jurisdiction to investigate her disappearance. But I remember Rebecca saying that her sister had lived here."

I supposed that made sense. I scooted closer to Hunter as three guys on bicycles practically plowed me down on the sidewalk.

Hunter gave them a dirty look as his gaze followed them, but he said nothing.

"Did you tell her to talk to the police here in Edgerton instead?" I asked, turning my attention back to Hunter.

"I told her if she was really worried, that's what she should do." He pressed his lips together before saying, "Her sister's past wasn't going to work in her favor, however."

"Past or not, justice is no respecter of color or socioeconomic status or past history, right?"

"Yes, that is true. However, I can see why local law enforcement may not be jumping on the chance to help."

"Rebecca thinks that the Beltway Killer may have grabbed her." Why did I keep blurting these things?

Hunter shook his head. "Whenever something goes wrong, people think the Beltway Killer did it. I can't tell you how many calls we get every week from people thinking that they've seen him or offering clues that lead nowhere."

"Really? I just assumed that there was no movement on the case." To read the news articles on it, the police weren't doing anything.

"The case is very fluid. The public doesn't get to know everything that we know."

I definitely thought I'd struck a nerve and decided to change the subject. "This building is one of the last addresses that Rebecca had for her sister. That's why I'm here."

"That's what I figured." Hunter frowned and glanced at the building again.

"So you've been here before for that reason?" My dad had always said I'd never been good at fishing. Little did I know he'd probably meant that literally and figuratively.

Hunter shrugged, as noncommittal as ever. "Maybe. But you don't know everything I know about Trina Morrison."

"What else is there to know?"

He stepped closer, the shadow in his gaze growing deeper. "Even though she doesn't live in Storm River anymore, she had quite the reputation as a party girl and all-around troublemaker. She could get into brawls with the best of them."

"Why do I have the feeling there's more you're not saying?"

He hesitated a moment longer before adding, "I strongly suspect that Trina beat up Rebecca once. When Rebecca came in to talk to us, I saw a fresh scar on the side of her face.

I asked her how she got it, but she wouldn't tell me. Only said she got into it with someone."

"You think that person was Trina?"

He nodded. "I do. She's dangerous. Rebecca wouldn't admit it or press charges, but that's what my bets are on."

I'd had no clue, but knowing that changed my perspective on Trina . . . for the worse.

The detective glanced at his watch before pulling his gaze back up to mine. "Look, I'm officially off the clock. What do you say you and I go grab some coffee?"

A surprising surge of excitement rushed through me. "I guess I could do that."

I didn't want to sound overly excited about it. Besides, I was supposed to be investigating. But maybe the detective would share something with me that would give me some insight into this case.

A girl could hope, at least.

THREE STREETS OVER, the town transitioned from low income and crime-ridden to trendy and artsy. The area was still on the edge of dangerous, but the colorful murals on the sides of the buildings and the trendy restaurants somehow made it more welcoming.

Detective Hunter had walked with me to a place called Bottoms Up. It was a coffee and tea house, and the people here seemed to know him. He led me to an empty table, and we sat down.

A moment later, the waitress took our orders. I got a decaf coffee, though I had little hope it would taste any good. Since I'd moved here, I'd yet to find any coffee that matched that from Yerba.

After the waitress left, Hunter turned toward me and got straight to the point. "You don't want to dive into the Trina Morrison case."

"So you admit that it's a case?"

He clucked his tongue and pointed his finger at me in a gotcha motion. "Uh huh. I keep feeling like you're trying to catch me."

"And I keep feeling like you're trying to discourage me."

"That's probably because I am." He leaned across the table, and his gaze locked with mine. "You don't know what you're getting into."

"Someone needs to help her. Is that why you're here?"

His gaze remained steady, not revealing a single thing. "I didn't say I was working this case. I'm just saying I know enough about Trina and her past to know that someone like you doesn't need to be jumping into this."

I leaned back. "Someone like me?"

What exactly had he meant by that? What exactly was I like? Ravishingly beautiful? Probably not. Totally brilliant? Not really. Fun to be around? Man, I couldn't even say that.

He frowned. "Don't read too much into that. I'm just

saying that I don't want to see you get hurt."

There was definitely more to this. If the detective wasn't working Trina's case, then what was he doing down here? I had so many questions that he'd probably never answer.

The server brought us our coffees, and I took a sip. The earthiness of the drink washed over my taste buds, and my eyebrows shot up.

"Do you like it?" Hunter watched me, almost as if he wanted this coffee to surprise me, to please me.

"I do. I've been called a coffee snob, but I have to say this stuff is pretty good."

A smile stretched across his face. "I always recommend this place to people."

"How do you know this area so well? I assumed you live in Storm River." I knew it wasn't any of my business, but I asked anyway.

"I've lived all over the DC area." He didn't offer any more information.

I was curious about this man. But he was a closed book. And we didn't have the kind of relationship that allowed me to dive into questions. Even this coffee meeting right now . . . it was nothing more than Hunter trying to discourage me from going into that apartment building.

I was smart enough to know that.

"How long do you plan on working for Oscar?" Hunter asked, taking a sip of his coffee.

The two men couldn't stand each other, but I still didn't

know why. I mean, I could see why Hunter wouldn't like Oscar. The man was a jerk. But something had happened between them that had left a lot of bad blood.

"I don't know," I admitted. "I thought I'd had my future planned out, but everything was turned upside down. I'm just trying to learn the ropes right now."

"Then why not try to do it in a professional way? We have an upcoming police academy session that's about to start. Why don't you apply?" He stared at me, waiting for my answer.

I'd never thought of myself as police material, nor did I ever think I would do fieldwork. I'd always assumed I was more of an administrator.

But as soon as I started working for Oscar and he had me do all the footwork for him, I discovered another side of myself. A side that was bolder. More courageous. Maybe even good at this.

"I'm just not sure I can see myself in a uniform," I finally answered.

"At least you would have some training under your belt before Oscar sent you out to the piranhas." His head tilted to the side as he waited for my reaction.

That sounded like an expression I would use. I was trying to break myself of the habit of using jungle analogies, but it was as hard as paddling upstream on the Amazon.

See?

"Where are you from?"

I told him about moving here from Yerba and how homesick I was. He nodded, a good listener. Or maybe this was his secret plot to catch me in a lie or a "gotcha!" moment. I'd just started telling him about being hired by Oscar when his phone buzzed.

He excused himself and put the device to his ear. A moment later, he returned to the table, a new shadow in his gaze.

"I'm sorry, but I've got to go." He pulled out his wallet and dropped a bill on the table. "It's on me."

The server had given us to-go cups so I grabbed mine. I wasn't ready to give up the rest of this coffee. Not considering it was the best I'd had since I left Yerba. I followed Hunter as he stepped onto the sidewalk and headed toward the apartment building where I'd parked.

He walked with me until we reached my vehicle and he saw I was safely inside. Before he closed my door, he peered down at me. "It was good to talk to you today, Elliot."

He remembered my name. I wasn't sure if that was a good or a bad thing. Did I want to be on a first name basis with the police?

"You too," I added.

He shut my door and hurried down the sidewalk. I knew he fully expected me to pull away. But I had at least thirty more minutes of daylight.

I glanced at the apartment building. I was already here, so I might as well go inside, right?

CHAPTER FIVE

IF THERE WAS one thing I'd learned about investigating, it was that you had to try to look like you blended in. People could get away with amazing things simply by looking like they belonged. That was what I needed to do now.

Michael had taught me that.

Then again, so had my dad. If you ever were about to get trampled by a wild herd of llamas? Roll in their turds, and they would think you were one of them. Clever, huh? I was sure there was a life lesson buried deep within the sage advice somewhere.

With that thought in mind, I pulled my hair back into a harsh ponytail and took off my jean jacket, revealing a black tank top. I also grabbed some lipstick from my purse and put it on extra thick. This was the last place I wanted to look like a good churchgoing girl.

I prepped myself mentally as I sat in the car, trying to get myself into the right mindset. I just needed to pretend that I was back in Yerba about to take a jungle hike, even though I knew there were jaguars lurking close, ready to pounce if I wasn't careful.

Keith Freddie lived on the third floor in apartment 328. I just needed to get there, ask him a few questions, and then I could be done.

I drew in a deep breath before climbing from my car. My first test would be getting past the two guys at the front door. I could feel their eyes on me as I approached, and one of them let out a low whistle. I pretended I didn't hear him and kept my gaze focused.

Just as I almost reached the door, one of the men grabbed my arm. "I don't think I've seen you around here before."

I made sure that my gaze looked razor sharp and cut into him. "Your point?"

A smile spread across his face when he heard the attitude in my voice. "Oh, you're a spicy mama. I like that."

"Don't touch me." I kept my voice hard, knowing I'd be fed to the piranhas Hunter had mentioned if I didn't.

He raised his hands. "Okay, okay. I hear you. Do your business, girl."

My lungs still felt tight as I pulled the door open and stepped inside. As soon as I was separated from those two men, I felt a rush of courage. I'd made it past my first obstacle okay. Hopefully, that was a good sign for what was to come.

I moved toward the stairs in front of me. Everything appeared yellow, but not because it had been painted that way. There were water stains in various places, and it smelled a bit like urine and nicotine.

This wasn't the place I would want anyone I loved to live. That was for sure.

I passed the second floor, and, as I did, I heard music blaring down the hallway, as well as voices. I kept moving.

Finally, I reached the third floor. Now I just needed to find Keith and ask him a few questions. I would be in and out like a squirrel monkey stealing food from a tourist on a picnic.

As I pulled open the door leading to the third-floor hallway, my throat tightened yet again. Numerous people lingered in the corridor. A couple people smoked something, which I was certain wasn't legal. And what they were smoking didn't smell like cigarettes either.

They didn't seem to care. But they all did seem to care about my presence there. The conversation stopped, and everyone stared at me as I stood there.

Keep your chin up, Elliot. Look like you belong.

I added a little swagger to my steps as I started down the hallway. I made sure not to make eye contact. I wouldn't speak unless I was spoken to. That wasn't exactly a rule I'd been taught, but it seemed like a good idea in this situation.

Had my father done things like this all the time? I'd had no clue my father had lived a clandestine life, and I still didn't know what to think about it. I liked to think I had some of his spy-worthy qualities inside me.

A couple people muttered things as I passed, but I chose to ignore them. I was certain I really didn't want to know what they said anyway.

Finally, I saw the door labeled 328. I didn't hesitate before knocking. I didn't want anyone around me to see even a hint of uncertainty in me.

Now I just hoped that Keith was home.

To my relief, the door opened a moment later, and a man stood there. He was a tall white guy with messy hair and more tattoos than Michael had. Something about his long hair and black T-shirt gave off a rock star look.

Or, should I say, a rock star wannabe look?

Wait . . . was that eyeliner? Did guys wear that?

He stared at me with squinty eyes, looking like I'd just woken him up.

"What do you want?" he barked over the sound of death metal music in the background.

"I need to talk to you about Trina."

His eyes narrowed. "I don't have anything to say about her."

"Please," I started. "It's important."

"What could be so important about Trina?" He attempted to toss a crushed-up beer can into a trash can across the room, but he missed. Instead of a groan, he let out an obnoxious belch.

"Please, I just need a moment of your time," I said.

He stared at me, his eyes cold, but finally he gave an ever so slight nod and stepped back. I took that as a sign I could go in, and I paced just inside the doorway.

I didn't need to go any deeper into his messy apartment. I didn't need to sit and have coffee. I just wanted to ask him a few questions alone.

I quickly noted an amplifier on the floor and an electric guitar in the corner.

It looked like my guess was right. This guy was a musician.

"People are worried about Trina," I started. "She hasn't been heard from in three weeks, according to my sources."

Keith let out a deep, sarcastic laugh. "Who's worried about her?"

"A friend."

"Trina doesn't have any friends."

"Why do you say that?"

"Because Trina doesn't care about anyone but herself."

"Is that right?" It hurt my heart to hear him say those words, especially since I'd seen so much affection in Rebecca.

But what if what Hunter had told me was true? If Trina really had gotten into a fight with her sister and left that scar on her face, then there was a lot more to this than I'd guessed.

"Do you have any idea where Trina is now?" I continued.

He shrugged. "Don't know. Don't care."

I glanced around and saw some pictures on his table. Pictures of him in front of a red, jacked-up truck. Pictures of him and Trina together. I had a hard time believing he didn't care.

I decided to try a different approach. "How about this then—when was the last time you saw her?"

"Four weeks ago." He picked up a couple crushed beer cans from the floor and attempted to toss them into the trash can. He missed again but made no move to clean up his mess. "This is what I know about Trina."

He stared, all his attention focused on me. I wasn't sure if that was a good thing or not, but I was going to have to live with it for the time being.

"Go on," I encouraged.

"Trina is selfish, and she never thinks of anybody but herself. Trouble goes wherever Trina goes. If you're smart, you won't look for her either."

"So you feel certain that she's okay?"

"Okay?" He snorted. "I never said anything about her being okay. But nothing was okay with her far before she supposedly disappeared."

"Keep going." I crossed my arms as I waited.

He shrugged. "I don't know what else to tell you. Like I said, the last time I saw Trina was about four weeks ago. She came home wearing all this new jewelry, broke up with me, and she left."

"Did she take her things with her?"

Something darkened in his gaze. "No. She left with just what she was wearing."

"And you didn't find that strange?" What kind of woman did that? My guess? A desperate one.

"Maybe a little. But like I said, Trina is unpredictable. I was just happy to have her gone from my life. I was so happy, in fact, that I burned everything she left."

"You burned it?" Certainly, I hadn't heard right. That seemed so . . . dramatic.

But based on the sparkle in his eyes, I had. "That's right. It's all ashes now. Good riddance." He raised his hands in the air, index and pinky finger raised, and he stuck his tongue out of his mouth.

Was that some kind of rocker thing? He looked ridiculous.

And his actions seemed extreme to me.

On the other hand, burning everything Sergio had given me might have been tempting at one time in my life. Still, I probably would have never done it.

"Why were you so happy to have her gone?" That sounded suspicious to me within itself. Was Keith so anxious to see Trina leave that he'd done something to her?

"Like I said, she was trouble. Always bringing new people around. Getting in cat fights."

"Cat fights?"

"That's the kind of person you're looking for—someone

who lashes out. Last time I saw her, her lip was busted. She told me someone tried to cut her in line, and they started to go at it right there in the grocery store."

"Really?" That seemed like an overreaction.

"Really. I'm trying to get myself clean. I just got a new job down at the docks that I can work when I'm not playing my gigs. I thought Trina would be proud, but she had no interest in the changes I was trying to make."

I glanced around the pigsty he called his apartment. "Trying to get yourself clean, huh?"

He shrugged. "I know this doesn't look like much to someone like you, but it's a start. Soon as I save up enough money, I'm going to get out of here. Speaking of which, you should probably get out of here too. Someone like you coming in here . . . you're just asking for trouble."

I couldn't argue with him there.

"If you think of anything else, can you call me?" I pulled out a card and left it on the table. Oscar had just had them made for me, and I'd picked them up Sunday after church.

"Yeah, sure thing. And my band is playing next week down at Cisco's." He handed me a flyer. "You should come. Tell your friends."

Just as I opened the door to let myself out, I heard someone yell, "Police!"

And then a whole army of SWAT soldiers invaded the apartment complex.

"PUT your hands against the wall! Everybody! Now!" the officers yelled as they rushed down the hallway.

My entire body seized with fear. What had I walked into? Was this the call that Hunter had gotten, taking him away from the coffee we'd been having together?

I'm not ready to die, and I think that I might cry. So please help me out here. Help me overcome fear. Right now is when, as I say amen.

Had I just rhymed my prayer?

I really did have issues.

"Now!" one of the SWAT officers yelled.

Without wasting any more time, I did as he said. I pressed my hands against the grimy cement walls in front of me. Keith did the same, muttering things I couldn't understand beneath his breath.

"What's going on?" I whispered.

"Drug raid," he said. "Just do as they ask and you should be fine. Probably."

It was that *probably* that had me shaken to my core. Hunter had known what he was talking about when he told me not to come here today, but I had been too stubborn to listen.

Another one of my not so fine qualities.

I waited, trembling, as I listened to the police move

behind me. As I waited, my mind was transported back to Yerba. To the political unrest that had happened there.

In the months right before my family had moved, much of the country was in a police state. A few times, I'd been afraid for my life. But my dad had always taken care of us.

Since I'd worked in politics, I was on the front lines. To some people, anyone who worked for the government was a target.

Right now, I heard the officers making their way down the hallway, talking to people. Yelling at them. Sounding, in general, like they were angry. I hated this so much. I couldn't be arrested just for being here . . . right?

Somebody stopped behind me. "Elliot?"

I knew without turning whose voice that was. I squeezed my eyes shut, wishing I could transport myself from this moment and the embarrassment that was sure to come. It was better if he didn't see my face.

"Hi, Detective Hunter," I finally said, still facing the wall.

He took my arm and turned me around, showing the stern look on his face. "I thought I told you not to come in here."

"I thought it was a suggestion."

He scowled and ran a hand over his face before leading me away. "No. It was because I knew a raid was about to happen. I'm part of an inter-city task force, and we've been working on this for weeks."

I shrugged. "Sorry. I figured, while I was already here, I might as well get the info I came for."

He stared at me, disbelief in his gaze. "And did you?"

I pressed my lips together, wishing I had more ammunition to justify my actions. "Not really. I mean, I did talk to Keith. But he doesn't know much."

Hunter led me down the stairs. He didn't stop walking until we reached my car. "This time I really am going to need you to get in your car and leave. Understand?"

I had no desire to stay here any longer so I nodded. "Understand."

He watched me get inside and close my door. He waited as I cranked my engine, and he was still standing on the sidewalk as I pulled away. I released the breath I'd held as the apartment building faded in my rearview mirror.

For now, I headed home. My mom and my sister should be there, and I hoped to catch up with them for a few minutes before going to bed.

I needed a little bit of normalcy to end my day.

CHAPTER SIX

AS I STEPPED into the office the next morning, panic fluttered through me. There was only one person who could help with my anxiety, and she was sitting right in front of me, giving herself a manicure and blowing oversized bubbles with her chewing gum.

"Velma." I rushed toward her desk and lowered my voice. "I have a date tonight."

Her eyes lit. "Is that right? How exciting. I found an old boutonniere in the trash last night. You want it for your man?"

"A boutonniere? Is that something that helps . . . button things?"

"No, it's—never mind. Go ahead."

"Okay. Anyway, he's not 'my man.' And the date isn't actually that exciting. I should have never said yes."

She stopped filing her nails and sat up, looking ready for some good gossip. "Why not?"

"I have nothing to wear, for starters."

"Certainly, you can find something."

She just wasn't getting this. "The last time this guy saw me, I was dressed like a million dollars in that dress you got for me to wear for the fundraiser. If I show up for dinner tonight wearing jeans and a black T-shirt, I'm not sure how that's going to go over."

"If he can't like you for who you are, then does it really matter if he likes you at all?" A new voice inserted itself into our conversation.

I turned and saw that Michael had breezed into the office.

I scowled and crossed my arms. "I don't really care if he likes me at all—"

"Then why does it matter what you wear?" Michael paused near me, a challenging look in his gaze.

"I guess I just realized that I set this guy up to think that he was going to go out with Fundraiser Elliot when in reality he's going to go out with Jungle Elliot."

"Jungle Elliot?"

I shrugged. "Let's face it. I'm more comfortable there than I am in a world where everything is supposed to look polished and perfect."

"Then maybe you should cancel," Michael said matter-of-factly.

I moved my arms from across my chest to my hips. "You really don't like this guy, do you?"

"I thought I'd made myself clear with that already. I make no secret about it."

"But what *is* a secret is why you don't like him." There was so much history between the people in this town. I just couldn't figure out Storm River dynamics. The curious part of me really wanted to.

Michael shook his head and started into the office the two of us shared. The change in conversation had him scurrying away. I supposed that was a good thing.

"There are some things I don't like to talk about," he muttered.

After he disappeared and closed the door, I leaned toward Velma. "What exactly happened between the two of them?"

I shouldn't ask, but I really wanted to know.

Velma sat up straighter and shrugged, a clueless look in her gaze. "Don't ask me. I have no idea. Now, back to your question. Do you remember that black shirt you wore last week? The one that had just a little bit of a ruffle at the bottom?"

"I do."

"Remember those ripped jeans that you wore that have a dark wash to them?"

"Yes, I only have one pair." My sister had helped me pick those out.

"And you have any heels maybe?"

"I have one pair of black heels."

"Perfect. That's what you're going to wear tonight. Put in some earrings." She narrowed her eyes as she studied me. "Leave your hair down. Unless he wants to take you someplace a little nicer. Then pull it back into some type of twist. Do you know where he's taking you?"

"He mentioned one of the seafood restaurants down at the harbor. Stockley's."

"That'll be a perfect look then. You've got this. You would look good in whatever you wore."

"I'm not really sure about that."

Before Velma and I could talk about it anymore, Michael emerged from his office with his keys in hand. "Come on, Elliot."

"We're leaving?" I'd just gotten here. I hadn't even visited my desk yet.

"We've got to go watch Burke again. Maybe today we'll actually see him do something he shouldn't be doing, and we can close the book on this investigation. If we could only be so lucky." Whatever bad mood Michael was in, it had carried over into today.

I didn't bother to argue. Instead, I cast one more look at Velma, and she shoved the box of donuts toward me.

At the last minute, I snatched one. I might need it later.

Then I followed Michael out to his minivan. Before we climbed in, Michael snatched the pastry from me and dropped it in the trash can. "From trash you were found and to trash you will return."

He had a point.

Still, it was quiet inside as we started down the road.

I didn't know what to say, and I didn't want to set Michael off. Not that he was the angry type. I didn't think he was, at least. I hadn't seen any hints of it.

"Look, I'm sorry," he started. He ran a hand over his face. "Jono always makes me a little cranky. And you're a nice girl. I don't want to see you get mixed up with someone like him."

"You have very strong feelings about this."

"I don't want to plant any ideas in your head. But I know you're smart, and I know you'll figure it out."

That wasn't what I wanted to hear. I wanted to know his thoughts. To hear his stories. To have some heart-to-heart time where he told me how he really felt.

Those desires made me realize that I desperately missed having a girlfriend to chat with. Michael hadn't volunteered for that position. But he was here, and we had nothing but time to kill.

"Look, the truth is . . . I'm going out with Jono because . . ."

Michael glanced over at me, waiting. Thankfully, I stopped myself before I said too much.

"Yes?" he said.

I couldn't tell him that the real reason I wanted to go out with Jono was because he had muttered something in

Spanish—*mantente alerta*—a phrase my father had always used. I wanted to know if he was somehow connected with my time in Yerba.

And maybe even with my father's death.

It sounded ridiculous. I knew it did.

But why would Jono have said those words the first time we met? And how could I explain the feeling that I was being followed? I had so many unanswered questions, and going out on a date with Jono meant that maybe I could find some answers.

"It's just because I'm trying to get back into the dating scene," I finally said, glancing out the window at Storm River as it blurred past. "What better way than by going out with somebody that I have no future with?"

Michael's eyes narrowed. "That's quite some logic you have there."

I shrugged and shook my head. "Look, it's not like that. I'm not the type to casually date. Not usually. But I've been all out of sorts since I moved here from Yerba and..."

"And what?"

I didn't know. "I ... don't feel like myself."

We parked near Burke's house and saw the man's car in the driveway. Burke stepped out of the front door just about the time we pulled up, a cell phone to his ear. He picked up a newspaper from his front sidewalk before going back inside. At least we knew he was home.

"How old are you?" Michael asked, the conversation obviously still on his mind. "You're what? Twenty-seven? Twenty-eight?"

"Twenty-seven."

"You ever been married?"

"No. Did you really think that I had?" I thought he knew me better than that.

"No, but I know many people your age who have already been married and who are no longer married. You seem like the marrying type."

I wasn't sure if he meant that as a compliment or an insult, but I was going to go with the compliment.

"I almost got married," I offered. Now why had I shared that? It wasn't something that I liked to talk about. As in ever. Those times were only bad memories now.

"Who was the lucky guy?"

I stared out the window for a moment, willing myself not to be transported back in time. "His name was Sergio."

"Sergio?" Michael's eyebrows shot up. "Sounds like a good Latino lover type of name."

He made a little rolling sound with his tongue that I never wanted to hear again.

"Latino lover?" I raised my eyebrows this time. "That's a little dramatic."

Michael crossed his arms and leaned back, as if ready for a good story. "So what happened between you two?"

I really didn't want to get into this. This was the problem with having so much time to kill while we waited for this man to do something that he might not ever do. I couldn't even feign an appointment. We were stuck here together.

"It's a long story," I muttered.

"I've got nothing but time."

I let out a sigh. "There's really not much to say. Sergio and I dated for about six months, and then he proposed. We talked about running off to get married and skipping the whole big wedding thing. And then, one day, I got a text from him saying that he wanted to call things off."

Michael flinched. "Ouch."

"Yeah, ouch is right." I fought back tears. I'd been certain I hadn't read those words correctly. In fact, I'd stared at the text for almost thirty minutes until I'd realized the reality of what Sergio had said.

"Did he ever explain himself or did he just leave you high and dry?" Michael was entirely more interested in this story than I thought he would be.

Sometimes, the breakup still felt fresh. I was over Sergio —I thought. So why did the hurt still linger like the aftertaste of eating an overcooked Guinea pig?

"He never explained himself. It was just like our whole relationship had never happened. Not even our relationship romantically. Or our friendship. After that, it was like I didn't exist and I meant nothing to him."

"He ghosted you?"

"Ghosted me? Is that the same as haunting someone?" Was Michael the superstitious type?

Michael shook his head. "No, it means someone stops returning your calls and texts."

What strange terminology. "Then, yes, I suppose he ghosted me."

"And you still had to see him after he called things off?"

I shifted, wondering why we had to have this highly uncomfortable conversation. Michael seemed like an expert at avoiding questions like this. Me? Not so much.

"That's right," I said. "I had to work with him every day."

"You dated a coworker?" He raised his eyebrows, as if that realization shocked him.

I felt my cheeks heat, a sure giveaway every time I got nervous. "No, it was even worse."

"How so?"

"The person I was going to marry, the one who grew wary . . . it was an even bigger loss . . ."

"Why's that?"

I swallowed hard. "Because I was dating . . . my boss."

CHAPTER SEVEN

MICHAEL STARED AT ME, something growing in his gaze. Curiosity? Maybe. Surprise? Definitely.

"Wait . . . I thought you worked for a legislator," he muttered.

"I did." I rubbed my hands together and stared out the window. I knew exactly where this conversation was going.

He sat up straighter. "So you worked for a legislator in your province, and then you ended up engaged to him?"

I rubbed my throat, wishing I could forget. "That's right. However, when he broke up with me, he transferred me to a different office."

"Ouch. Without telling you?"

I raised my chin as the memories rushed at me like a bull at a rodeo. "That's correct. No one knew, though. We kept our relationship a secret."

"Secret from who?" Michael turned toward me, and I realized I had his full attention.

I didn't really want his full attention right now, though. I wanted to hide under a rock—even if there were centipedes and beetles there with me.

"We kept it a secret from . . . everybody." My throat tightened as bad memories filled me.

"Even from your parents?"

"Especially my parents." I wasn't proud of my actions. But I'd listened to logic for so long. It felt good to listen to my heart. But it had been a mistake.

Just like my parents had said.

A smile spread across his face, and he nodded with satisfaction. "So Elliot Ransom does have a rebellious side to her."

"It wasn't my finest moment, but I knew my father would not approve. In fact, at first, we weren't going to keep it quiet. Sergio even came over to my house a few times for dinner. But once my parents said they didn't approve, we broke it off. Only to get back together. But we didn't tell anyone. I was convinced my parents were wrong and that I knew best."

"Why didn't your father approve?"

"My father also worked for the government. He knew Sergio, and he didn't like him."

"Why didn't he like him?"

Michael was just full of questions, wasn't he? If the tables were turned right now, I was confident he wouldn't be so chatty.

"Let's just say the two of them didn't agree politically speaking. Sergio was on the side of reforming the government, and my dad was on the side of wanting it to remain what it had always been. The old and the new clashed."

"Where did you stand?"

I glanced at my hands again. Michael had no idea how deep these questions ran. Unless someone had been in my shoes and seen their home country implode, they couldn't understand. "Initially, I wanted things in my country to remain the way they were. After all, it was the way I'd been raised. But as I listened to Sergio's views, they were very convincing."

"But that's what led to all of this uprising, correct?" Michael put the pieces together. "The old versus the new."

I nodded. "It actually went much deeper than I thought it did. Looking back now, I can see a little more clearly. The people who were in power, the people who were supporting the incumbent president . . . they were blindsided by Xavier Flores, the man who eventually overthrew the leadership— the old guard, as some people called it. He was nothing but corrupt and evil."

"What happened to Sergio?"

"Last I heard, he's in the new president's cabinet. All his backstabbing paid off." I couldn't stop the frown from pulling at my lips.

Michael let out a whistle. "Wow."

"I know. I feel for all the people I left behind, and I wish that there was some way that I could help them." We'd been so fortunate to get out when we did, before the militia took over, patrolling the streets and enacting their own laws. They instilled fear in people in order to get what they wanted.

"And there's the real Elliot Ransom." Michael clucked in tongue. "The girl who wants to help everybody. True fact."

I shrugged. "I don't want to help everybody. Sometimes I don't even think I can help myself."

Michael's gaze softened as his inquisitiveness faded. "I think you're doing pretty well, Elliot."

"Thanks," I told him.

Part of me wanted to ask him about his dating life. But I would need to save that conversation for another day. First, I needed to decompress.

FOUR HOURS LATER, Nolan Burke still hadn't left his house.

I turned to look at Michael, feeling like I needed a nap. "How long are we going to do this?"

"Until he messes up."

"But what if he doesn't mess up? What if he's telling the truth?"

I was going to lose my mind. I'd already read a book,

written out my life goals for the next three months, deleted old pictures on my phone, and arranged the rest of the photos in folders.

Michael shrugged and stretched his arms. He'd been playing some kind of game on his phone for the past couple hours. "I know the company is paying us to do this for at least a week."

"That can't be cheap." I couldn't see where the payoff would be worth it.

"It's still cheaper than paying out tens of thousands of dollars for this guy's medical bills and the therapies he claims he's going to need."

"But what if he's innocent?" Why were they so certain this man was lying?

"They must have their reasons to suspect that he's not if they're paying all this money."

I leaned back in my seat. Maybe this wasn't the career for me.

My mind drifted back to Rebecca Morrison. Maybe I could keep myself occupied by planning out my next steps in that investigation. It seemed better than nothing.

Last night, I'd done some research based off my conversation with Keith. I really wanted to go and talk to Trina's best friend today. However, between work and my date with Jono, I wasn't sure I was going to have time.

Which was a problem.

Finally, at two o'clock, Burke left his house. A spike of

excitement went through me when I saw him climb into his car. At least, that meant Michael and I didn't have to sit here anymore.

"Change of scenery, here we come," Michael said, starting up his minivan.

We kept a safe distance behind Burke as he traveled down the road. When he headed out of town, I wondered exactly where he was going. Probably nowhere exciting, knowing our luck.

"Let's just hope he's doing something stupid right now," Michael said.

Fifteen minutes later, Burke pulled up to a movie theater. After parking, he climbed out of his car, met a friend, and they walked inside together.

Disappointment gripped me. "So much for that one, huh?"

Michael sighed and glanced at his watch. "I think we can probably call it a day. By the time the movie's over, we're practically going to be off work."

I glanced at my phone and realized we were only five minutes away from Trina's best friend's place. "While we're up this way . . . what do you say we make a quick stop?"

"Where could you possibly want to go up here?"

"I would like to talk to somebody named . . ." I glanced at my screen. "Shawna White."

"Who is Shawna White?"

Michael just *had* to ask all these questions, didn't he? It was almost like he was an investigator or something.

"She was best friends with Trina Morrison, if you must know." He was going to get that info out of me one way or another, so I might as well be direct.

Instead of driving away from the movie theater, Michael pulled into a parking spot and put the van into Park. "Wait . . . you're still looking into this?"

I shrugged. "I figure it can't hurt to poke around for some answers."

He waved his finger in the air. "That's where you're wrong. It can definitely hurt."

"I didn't say I was going to do anything stupid." Even as I said the words, I remembered being at that apartment complex last night when the police raid happened. I didn't need to mention that to Michael, however. He was already questioning my choices, and I didn't need to give him more ammunition.

"I just want to talk to her." Why did I feel like I was talking to my dad right now?

"Why is this so important to you?" Michael's gaze pierced mine.

"I don't know. It just seems a shame if no one helps her."

He let out a long breath, almost as if he was about to be pulled down into quicksand and felt helpless to stop it. "You said she thinks the Beltway Killer might be at play here?"

"That's what Rebecca thinks. Trina does fit the description of his victims."

"If the police thought that the Beltway Killer was involved with this, they definitely wouldn't ignore the fact that she's missing. You've got to know that, Elliot."

"I think part of the reason they're ignoring the fact that she's missing is because she has a history of being a trouble-maker. Trouble is as trouble does." My mom always said that, and the expression seemed to fit right now.

His gaze pierced even deeper. "Even more reason why you shouldn't be involved."

I wasn't ready to drop this. I needed to convince Michael to see things my way. "But what if she didn't just disappear on her own? She could be in trouble. What if she needs help?"

He let out another breath. "Let's just say the Beltway Killer is involved here. Do you really want to insert yourself into a situation with a serial killer?"

"At least I would get that reward . . ." Information leading to the Beltway Killer's arrest came with a hefty amount of money—money I could really use.

"The 100K?" His eyes narrowed. "And what could you possibly want that reward so bad for? You don't seem like the type who's all about money."

"I'm not. But my sister needs a double lung transplant. That takes a lot more money than you might think, even with insurance."

His gaze softened. "Double lung?"

"She has cystic fibrosis."

"That's a lot. I'm really sorry."

"Me too."

He shifted toward me, his voice still soft. "That said, I still don't think you should be involved here."

"And I appreciate your advice. However, I can swing by Shawna White's house now or I can go back past it later. I'm not going to make you do anything you don't want to do."

Michael stared at me for another moment before letting out a sigh. "I'll go with you. Only because I want to keep you out of trouble."

"I repeat, I'm not forcing you to do anything that you don't want to do," I reminded him. No way did I want him holding this over my head.

"Yeah, yeah," he muttered, putting his van into Drive. "Tell me where I'm going."

CHAPTER EIGHT

A FEW MINUTES LATER, Michael and I pulled up to a row of townhouses that had seen better days. Storm River was such a nice town, but everywhere I needed to go seemed to be eyesores in the area.

Michael put the van in Park in front of the building. I was so glad he was here with me. Everything always felt easier when he was around.

He pointed to the building with the dilapidated orange siding, junky porches, and broken fences. "There?"

I double-checked on my phone. "That's the place."

"You think this lady is around?"

"I have no idea. But what better way to find out than by asking, right?"

Michael climbed from the car, and I followed behind. We

walked beside each other up to Shawna's door and knocked. Black paint peeled on the edges of the panels there, and a faded bench sat out front. An old car battery sat on that bench, as well as a water hose spray nozzle, an old beer box, and three pairs of chopsticks.

There was no answer.

I knocked again. Still no answer.

"At least you didn't come all this way for nothing," Michael offered. "We were already in the area."

At least. But part of me was disappointed. It would be nice just to talk to one helpful person.

As we turned to leave, something on the ground caught my eye. It was a nametag with Shawna written on it. Below her name were the words "Sunset Grill."

I glanced at Michael. "It looks like she may have dropped this."

We had another clue, and I wasn't going to complain.

———

"LET ME GUESS. You want to go to the Sunset Grill now?" Michael turned to me as we climbed into his minivan.

"Only if you have time."

"Translation: yes, please." He glanced at the time on his console. "We can swing by quickly. Then I need to get home for Chloe."

"Thank you." I feared he might give me a hard time, but I was thankful he was onboard, however begrudgingly.

"Is there anything else interesting you've discovered in this case so far?"

"And why are you asking? Because you want part of the reward? Are you going to steal it from me?" My voice sounded teasing.

"Ouch." He glanced at me. "You really think I'm that kind of guy?"

"No, I think if you were that type of guy you wouldn't have taken a job with Oscar." Someone with Michael's skills could have easily gotten another position that paid better.

Michael nodded. "At least you give me credit for that."

"I did go out investigating yesterday. I didn't discover much, but I talked to Trina's ex-boyfriend. He said she just up and left one day."

"And?"

What else had Keith told me? "She left all her things."

"Do you think that's weird?"

"I think it's weird for anyone to leave all their stuff behind, even if they are a little bit flighty." I pointed up ahead. "My GPS is telling me that you need to turn here."

"What else do you know? If I'm getting involved, I need all the facts."

He was getting involved? That was the best news I'd heard all day. "I also discovered that Trina has a reputation for not only being flighty and irresponsible, but her sister has a scar on the side of her face that Trina gave her when she got upset with her one time."

Michael glanced at me before shaking his head. "Maybe she's not the kind of woman you want to find."

"She definitely doesn't sound like she should be receiving any gold stars for her behavior anytime soon."

"You have to use your critical thinking skills, Elliot. I know you have them. Does that make you question her character at all?"

"Some. But I'm just skimming the surface. I want to see what else I could figure out before I give up. *If* I give up."

"That sounds more like it. Don't chain yourself to this case."

I pointed again to where we needed to go, and, a few minutes later, we pulled up to a strip of shops that had seen better days. The whole building was outdated, with peach-colored bricks and crooked, faded signs above each of the four doors of the businesses. There was a laundry mat, a Caribbean restaurant, a vape shop, and then, finally, on the end there was the Sunset Grill.

"You take the lead, boss," Michael said.

"Great. That was exactly what I wanted." Or not. Despite that, I knew that this undertaking was my doing so I had no choice but to step up here.

We walked into the small hole-in-the-wall restaurant that had been set up almost like a diner. The place smelled like greasy burgers and crisp french fries.

I started to salivate but stopped myself.

I could not adopt the American diet. I'd been here only three months, and I could already feel my taste buds changing. I preferred to snack on mangos and pineapple—not grease-laden food. I needed to keep it that way.

An older woman wearing a pink uniform greeted us at the door and led us to a table. As she did, my gaze scanned the restaurant.

There appeared to be only one other waitress working. I couldn't get a glance at her nametag, but I really hoped it read Shawna.

The woman seemed to fit the right age category that would put her in the same generation as Trina. She had blonde hair that she wore in two sloppy buns just above her ears. She had a trendy look, especially with her thick eyeliner and red lipstick.

"What now?" Michael stared at me, almost as if he was testing me.

"Now? I need to see if that's our girl."

Just then, the woman started our way, pen and paper in hand. "Can I help you?"

I glanced at her nametag. It looked like the original name had been whited out, and she'd written "Shawna" in marker over it.

Bingo!

"Ma'am?" she repeated, holding her order pad.

I snapped back to reality and remembered that I had ten whole dollars in my wallet. "I will have an orange juice."

The woman's gaze fluttered up to mine before she turned to Michael. "And you?"

"I'll take a burger, fries, and a Coke."

She grinned at him, a flirty smile crossing her lips. "I like a man who knows how to eat and can stay fit."

I resisted an eye roll—and I hoped he wasn't expecting me to pay for his meal.

Shawna winked at Michael. "Your order will be right up."

"Excuse me—" Before I could finish, Shawna walked away, calling out the order to someone in the kitchen.

Amusement danced in Michael's eyes. "This is no time to use your introvert voice."

"When you ordered a full-out lunch, it threw me off, as did her blatant flirting." I was using a diversion tactic and trying to fling the attention back on him.

"I thought this was your treat." His eyes sparkled.

"Then you obviously have no idea how my mind works—or my wallet."

He chuckled. "No, believe me. I do. I'll pay for my own. You have it planned out what you're going to ask this lady?"

"In administrative terms, I love planning and organizing. Relationally? Not so much. I like conversations to happen naturally."

"Hmm . . . we'll see how that works," Michael said. "It's risky."

"I have a feeling you're doubting me."

He rubbed the cross tattoo on his finger. "I didn't say anything about doubting. I've been teaching you some skills over the past several days. Now I'm just going to watch you put them into practice, my little grasshopper."

I stared at him.

"Never mind. It's from a classic TV show, *Kung Fu*."

"Very well then. I'll give this a go again." I flinched. I'd rhymed again. I hadn't even meant to that time.

A few minutes later, Shawna reappeared with Michael's food and our drinks.

"Here you go. Enjoy, and let me know if you need anything else." She winked at Michael.

"Actually," I called. "I do need something else. I'm a friend of Trina's, and I was wondering if you'd seen her lately."

Shawna looked at me as if she didn't believe me. Rightfully so. "*You* knew Trina?"

I shrugged. "Is that hard to believe?"

She looked at me like a butcher sizing up meat. "You don't look like the type that Trina would hang out with."

Should I be insulted? "And what is that type?"

She pursed her lips as she continued to observe me. "You look all innocent and Goody Two-Shoes. Trina is trouble. If you don't know that, then you don't know Trina."

I lowered my voice. "The truth is, someone asked me to look for her."

Shawna glanced at Michael then me. "So you're cops?"

"No, we're not cops," I told her. "We work for a PI."

She shrugged and took a step back. "I don't know what you want me to tell you."

"Just anything that you might know about Trina," Michael said. "About how we might be able to find her."

Shawna seemed to soften as Michael said the words. She shrugged, some of her edginess disappearing. "I don't know where Trina is. I haven't talked to her in a couple weeks. We had a falling out."

"It seems like Trina had a falling out with a lot of people," Michael continued.

Trina really wasn't likable, was she?

"You can say that again. I'm not sure what happened to her, but she got a big head. Suddenly, she thought she was too good for all of us." Shawna rolled her eyes.

"Why do you say that?" I asked.

Shawna bristled as she glanced at me. Then she looked back at Michael as she answered. "She came by one day and talked about how she had a new job opportunity. She was wearing all this fancy new jewelry, practically gloating about it. She'd moved out and away from Keith, and she told me that we probably wouldn't be talking for a while."

What had happened to cause that change? If I figured that out, maybe I'd finally start finding answers. "Did she say what this new job opportunity might be?"

Shawna glanced behind her, looking for customers—or a

way out. "She didn't say. She just said that it was a really good one."

"Did she say anything else that might give you a clue as to where we might find her?" Michael asked.

She shrugged. "I figured she had a new boyfriend. She didn't tell me that. It was just the way she acted. But I figured he was rich and that's where Trina got her jewelry. But he must have been mean also."

"Why do you say that?" I asked.

"Because she had some bruises on her arm. Maybe she thought the pain was worth it." Shawna shrugged. "Different strokes for different folks."

It seemed a little callous to me, but I understood that this was a hard situation. "Anything else that might help us?"

Shawna stared out the window a moment before turning back to us. "She said something about Riverside."

"What's Riverside?"

"It's a condo complex about ten minutes from here," Michael said. "It's pretty upscale."

"So this new job must have paid pretty well." I nodded, as a better picture began forming in my mind.

Shawna scowled. "That's how Trina made it sound. I guess she had moved on and moved up, and her old friends were no longer good enough for her. But that was always her goal. She likes to use people to get ahead. I always told her she should be rich because she would fit right in with those kinds of people."

Ouch. Her words weren't kind. Then again, most of what people said about Trina wasn't kind.

"Thanks for your help. If you think of anything else, can you call me?" I slid my card to her.

"Don't count on it. I don't want anything to do with that woman. Not after she dropped me like a bad Tinder date."

CHAPTER NINE

I'D NOTICED Michael glancing at his phone several times during our conversation, and I figured he must have gotten an important text. As soon as we climbed into his minivan, he updated me.

"I've got to get Chloe to soccer practice. My mom's in a meeting that's running overtime. Do you mind if we swing by the school to pick her up, and then I can drop you at your car?"

I had to admit I was a little excited about meeting Chloe. I'd heard so much about her. "Sure thing. That's no problem."

"Good thing you agree. Otherwise, I'd have to abduct you. True fact." He flashed a smile.

"If you did, I'd have to use some Yerbian feather torture on you."

He raised an eyebrow. "Feather torture?"

"Believe me, you don't want to know."

He let out a chuckle. "No, I have a feeling I don't."

As we took off down the road, Michael glanced over at me and asked, "Did you get the information you wanted?"

"I'm not sure if I got the information I wanted or not, but at least I now have somewhere else to look. And Shawna certainly liked you."

"She's a flirt."

I wondered if Michael got that reaction a lot. I supposed the more I got to know him, the more I would figure that out.

A few minutes of silence fell between us.

"Did you have any thoughts on this investigation?" I asked.

Michael shrugged. "I am curious about this new job that Trina got that allowed her to live up in Riverside. Lots of young professionals from DC like to live there."

"Trina's skills before this were waitressing and working at a gas station," I said. "I wonder what kind of upgrade she was able to find. A rich, new boyfriend?"

"That's a great question," Michael said. "I can't tell you. But it will be interesting to discover what it is."

Interesting was a good way to put it. I really hoped I hadn't gotten into something over my head. But I was getting in deep now, and I really wanted answers. I wanted to know what had happened to Trina. What had caused those changes. I also wondered if she was alive. I hoped for her sister's sake that she was.

A few minutes later, Michael and I were back in Storm River, and we pulled up to an elementary school. Michael pulled something out of his glove box, a little sign with a school bus on it and a number. He held it in his window as we got in a carpool line.

"So this is where Chloe goes to school, huh?" The place looked just as I expected. It matched all the other buildings here in Storm River with its pale gray siding, dormers, over-sized shutters, and white trim. Everything looked coastal and clean.

"It's a good school. It's one more reason I want to stay in this area. The teachers really are top-notch." He readjusted his hat as he stared off into the distance.

"And Chloe likes it here?"

"She has a lot of friends, and she loves my parents, so I can't complain."

We moved forward in the carpool line, and I watched as bouncy children with backpacks ran toward the vehicles in front of us and climbed inside with the help of a school employee.

A few minutes later, we pulled into the pickup area and a little blonde girl with freckles ran out to the car and opened the back door. I got a better picture of what Chloe's mom must have looked like because the girl looked nothing like Michael.

"Daddy, Daddy, Daddy! You're here." Chloe's gaze went to me, and she froze. "Who are you?"

At least the girl was direct.

"This is my coworker, Elliot. Elliot, this is Chloe."

"Hi, Elliot." Chloe put on her seat belt. "Nice to meet you. I've never met a girl named Elliot before."

"My mom named me after a famous missionary. An author named Elizabeth Elliot."

"Daddy told me about her before. Didn't she live in the jungle as a missionary?" Her voice lilted with curiosity.

I glanced at Michael, surprised by the fact he'd told Chloe that story. "That's right. That's where she worked for a lot of years."

"Well, it's nice to meet you, Elliot. Are you going to my soccer game?"

Chloe was absolutely precious. Three minutes into meeting her, I already knew that. Any seven-year-old who could talk to an adult with more finesse than most grownups was unforgettable.

"I don't think I'm going to be able to go to your soccer game," I told her. "But that sounds like a lot of fun."

"It is, Elliot," Chloe continued. "And my dad is coach. He's the best."

"Is that right?" I glanced at Michael. Something else he hadn't mentioned. I knew the man had been a professional baseball player before his career got sidelined by some bad choices.

"He is the best coach ever," Chloe continued.

"I think that's great."

I bet any single moms at those games gawked over their single dad coach. I wondered if Michael ate up that attention or if he pretended he didn't notice. I remembered his reaction to Shawna—he'd been polite yet he hadn't led her on.

I would bet that was his normal.

"So how was school today, honey?" Michael asked, glancing into the backseat.

"It was okay, but Judas Mulberry threw up all over the table in the cafeteria, and it was so gross. All the boys were pointing at it and making jokes while all the girls were screaming. I almost think the boys liked that we were grossed out."

"You think boys like stuff like that?" Michael smiled.

"Yes. Absolutely."

I glanced back in time to see Chloe make a face, and I couldn't blame her. Boys could definitely be gross.

"So how do you like working with my dad?" Chloe asked.

She sure was a talker. It made me wonder if Chloe's mom was also a talker. Michael didn't like to say very much about her, but I was curious.

"I think your dad is a very smart man," I finally said as I shifted to better see her. "He's really taught me a lot. But we've only been working together for less than two weeks."

"My dad is super smart. He has been teaching me how to

shoot a bow and arrow, and this summer he said he would teach me how to drive a boat."

"Is that right? My dad used to teach me all kinds of stuff too." My heart panged with a moment of sadness.

"Like what?"

My mind raced back in time to when life had seemed so carefree, back when I'd thought my family would be intact forever and that I'd live the rest of my days in Yerba. "Well, he taught me self-defense so, in case I got in trouble, I would know how to fight back."

Chloe's eyes widened. "That seems like a good thing to know."

"Oh, it's definitely good to know."

"What else did he teach you?" Chloe leaned forward as far as her seatbelt would allow.

"Chloe, you don't want to overwhelm Elliot with all your questions," Michael said.

"Oh, it's no problem," I said. "Like I said, my dad taught me lots. Aside from self-defense, he also taught me that when I got scared, I could come up with rhymes."

"How do rhymes help you when you get scared?" Her lips twisted into a confused frown.

"Well, it keeps your thoughts busy. When we let fear invade our every thought, it can take over our bodies too. So if we can focus on something else, it can help us get through scary moments."

"That's also a method used for PTSD," Michael said.

I wondered how he knew about that, but I knew this wasn't the time to ask. "My dad liked to teach me a lot of life skills, like how to survive in the jungle, for instance."

"The jungle?" She giggled. "Why would you need to know that?"

"Because I grew up in the jungle."

"Did you? I've always wanted to go to the jungle. Just like Dora."

Funny that she brought up Dora the Explorer. When Oscar and I had first met, he liked to call me that. I hadn't realized at the time that it was a subtle insult.

Before Chloe could ask any more questions, we pulled up in front of the office. This was my cue to leave so they could get to soccer.

It also meant that I needed to start getting ready for my date with Jono. Dread pooled in my stomach.

Before I opened my door, I turned back to Chloe. "It was really nice to meet you."

"It was nice to meet you too. I want to hear your jungle stories someday."

I smiled. "I would love to tell you the stories."

I glanced at Michael. As he looked at Chloe, his eyes glowed with love and affection for her. My dad had looked at me like that also.

Maybe it *would* be hard for Michael to find the right woman to date. A lot of females might be intimidated by how much he adored his daughter. But I thought it was a wonderful thing, something to be admired.

"Thanks for everything, Michael. I'll see you tomorrow."

"Have fun with dinner tonight." His voice changed to a low, unapproving tone again.

I still had so much to learn about everybody here in town.

Right now, I needed to focus on what I could learn about my father's untimely death. If he was murdered, then someone needed to pay.

Was that person Jono?

CHAPTER TEN

AFTER I GOT DRESSED, I looked in the mirror and nodded.

Velma might be a cheapskate, but she did have good taste. I'd put on the outfit that she'd suggested, and I had to admit it looked pretty good. The only thing I'd changed was that I had pinned my hair back, leaving a few loose tendrils. The look made me feel more sophisticated.

It was weird how moving to America had left me feeling so off balance. Back in Yerba, I'd had a career. I'd even rented my own apartment. I'd felt like I had everything figured out.

Then within the span of a year, everything had been turned upside down. Sometimes, I felt like I'd reverted back to my teenage years, those times when I was so uncertain about the future and who I was.

My security blanket was gone, and I was having to recalculate my entire life.

I glanced at my watch. I had just enough time to make it to my date. I'd told Jono that I would meet him at the restaurant.

Before I could hurry out the door, my mom stepped into the house still wearing her smock from the drugstore.

She'd always been a homemaker. But when my father passed, we'd been left with nothing. No life insurance policy. No savings.

It seemed so unlike my father to leave us in this position.

Knowing what I did now about his death, I had to wonder if there was some kind of connection between his passing and our total lack of funds.

Either way, it pained me to see my mom look so tired. But we were all doing whatever we could to get by. It required sacrifice, but that's what family did.

"Don't you look nice," she muttered, hanging her keys on a hook by the door.

"I have a date," I announced. I was already hiding my job situation, and my theory about my father's death, from her—which made me lose sleep at night. There was no need to hide this also.

Her eyebrows shot up. "With who?"

"You don't know him. His name is Jono."

She glanced at the keys in my hand. "He's not picking you up?"

"In this day and age, it's better if you don't give your home address out first." That was a true fact, as Michael liked to say.

Her eyes narrowed in disapproval. "Well, back in my days of dating, the boy had to meet the parents first."

"Did Dad meet your parents first?" I already knew the answer to that question. She'd met my dad in Yerba when she went over to become a missionary. They'd gotten married before her parents ever met him. I didn't mean to be passive aggressive but . . .

"That was different." She raised her chin.

I kissed her cheek and then grabbed my purse. "So is this. It's no big deal, just a little date."

"What's this guy's last name, just in case?"

"Harris," I answered.

Her eyes widened. "Is he related to the Harris family here in town?"

I paused. I honestly didn't think my mom was up on things like who the rich people in town were. "As a matter of fact, he is. How do you even know them?"

"His dad has come into the store a couple times. The other workers there talk about him, about how he's one of the richest men on the East Coast."

"I've heard rumors about something like that."

"I didn't realize that you like dating people like that." She studied my face, no doubt trying to figure out if she needed to rebuke me for embracing American culture too fast, too much, too . . . at all.

"I'm just trying to be more open-minded than I normally am. It's the only reason I'm going on this date. I don't see a future with him."

Worry stained my mother's gaze. "I understand— although you know how I feel about dating for fun. Dating should lead to marriage."

"First dates don't lead to marriage. First dates are to figure out if there will be a second date. I'm twenty-seven. You have to trust me sometime."

Mama gave me a "mom look" before nodding. "Fine. Have fun and be safe."

I nodded before hiking my purse up higher and opening the door to step outside. A few minutes later, I was heading down the road to the harbor area of Storm River.

The restaurant that Jono had chosen was actually not far from The Board Room Cafe. In fact, Stockley's Seafood was located right on the river, and apparently it had stunning views. I'd seen Jono in the area before, and I knew he had a yacht he docked nearby.

Nerves raced through me as I climbed out of my car.

As I glanced at the building, I straightened my shirt, ironing out imaginary wrinkles. "Here goes nothing."

I STILL FELT an unusual amount of nerves as I stepped into Stockley's. I didn't know what I'd been expecting with the restaurant, but I hadn't thought it would be as upscale as it was. Instead of little fishing knickknacks decorating the space, this restaurant had a whole wall of glass windows, sleek tables, and a glossy wooden floor. The lighting was dim, and soft music played overhead.

Oh, wait. That was live music. A pianist sat at a baby grand in the corner.

Maybe I was underdressed. I ran my hand over my outfit and briefly pondered if I had enough time to return home and change.

I knew I didn't.

As if to confirm that, I heard someone step up behind me. "Don't you look lovely, Elle?"

Elle? That's right. That's what I'd told Jono my name was. It was what my dad used to call me, and I'd used it as a cover on an assignment.

I turned and saw Jono standing there with a sparkling grin.

Yes, the one and only Jono Harris. Like I'd told my mom, he came from one of the wealthiest families on the East Coast. Old family money, I'd heard, though his father ran some type of corporation.

Also from what I heard, Jono didn't have to work. He mostly did what he wanted around town, which usually included frequent dating. Michael referred to those women as flavors of the month.

The man was nice-looking, there was no doubt about that. He had thick, dark hair that he wore gelled away from his face. His teeth were incredibly white. His clothes looked stylish, and I wasn't normally the type to ever even notice those things. But something about the man screamed rich. Screamed that he was a little different than everybody else, a little better. He probably liked it that way.

I forced a smile and reminded myself of why I was here—to find out information on my dad.

"Jono," I murmured, trying to put on my most cultured demeanor. Part of me thought of this as an assignment, thought of myself as an investigator digging deep for answers. "It's so nice to see you."

He leaned forward and brushed his lips against my cheek. "So nice to see you too." His hand remained on my arm. "I have a table picked out for us already."

I wondered if there was a table here reserved just for him and his dates. I wished I could say I was joking, but I wasn't. He was that type. Privileged and proud.

"This place is nice." I glanced around.

"It's not your first time here, is it?" He took my elbow and led me to our table.

He'd worn designer jeans, loafers, and a button-up shirt. Velma had nailed my outfit for this evening. Go, Velma!

"Actually, it is. I'm new to the area."

"I figured a girl like you would be here all the time."

This man obviously had a false impression of me. If he saw my car, he'd know the truth. In fact, in some ways, I felt a little bit like Cinderella. The very first time Jono and I had met, I had been broken down on the side of the road. The second time we'd met, I'd been dressed up at a nice fundraiser and looked like an entirely different person. The man hadn't even recognized me.

As we sat at the table with a little candle flickering in front of us, I glanced around.

There was that feeling again. The feeling that I was being watched.

But as I looked around, I didn't see any eyes on me.

No, I took that back. A couple people did glance my way. But I had the distinct impression they looked at me because I was with Jono, not because I was their prey.

Jono raised his hand, and, as soon as he did, a waiter appeared with a pad of paper in hand. I'd seen things like that happen before. It had been in Yerba and had mostly involved politicians with big heads who demanded, however subtly, that kind of service.

He ordered some shrimp cocktail for us before turning his full attention on me. "So, I have to admit that I've been thinking about you ever since we met at the fundraiser last week."

"Have you? I'm flattered." Truly, I was. This guy could probably date supermodels if he wanted.

He leaned closer, his eyes narrowing with curiosity. "You're a bit of a mystery. No one in town really knows much about you."

"Does that mean you've been asking around?" *That* didn't flatter me. It scared me. There were some things that were better left secret—like the fact I worked for Oscar.

He offered a charming shrug. "I guess I have. But don't worry—no one knows anything about you. So tell me about you."

I'd decided *not* to go with a cover story. Instead, I gave him a brief rundown of growing up in Yerba and then moving here. As he listened, I didn't see any type of recognition in his eyes, not a hint that anything I said sounded familiar or expected.

If he truly was someone with a connection to my father's past, then he had to already know part of my story, right? The only other thing I could figure was that I'd misunderstood him.

I'd felt certain that Jono had said those words in Spanish the first time I saw him.

Mantente alerta.

But I supposed he could have said something else and my mind had simply drawn different conclusions.

As we talked, the waiter brought us some water and bread along with our shrimp cocktails. Jono ordered a fish dinner with roasted potatoes and vegetables while I got a crab cake with rice pilaf. It didn't take long for our food to come out.

If I was able to forget about the fact that I felt like somebody was watching me and that I was suspicious of Jono, I might even enjoy this evening.

It wasn't that Jono and I had anything in common, but the man was obviously good at talking to people and making an impression.

As soon as the conversation turned from me, Jono began telling me about himself. About all the houses his family owned, which car was his favorite, and the best places he'd ever gone on vacation. His life was nothing like mine, but it was fascinating.

Just then, somebody wandered over toward us. An older man with graying hair who looked distinguished. I'd seen him somewhere before, but I couldn't place where yet.

"Mr. Harrington," Jono muttered. "This is Elle Ransom. She's new in town."

I nodded hello to the man, pretending I was at one of the political functions I'd attended in Yerba. "Nice to meet you."

"You too, Elle."

"Will you be playing at the benefit golf tournament next month?" Mr. Harrington asked Jono, turning his attention back to him.

"I was planning on it."

"Good. I was hoping you would say that. Nice to meet

you, Elle." Mr. Harrington looked back at me. "You should bring her with you."

"I would love to." Jono flashed one of his charming smiles my way.

I hadn't scared the man off yet. Then again, I hadn't used any of my jungle analogies or broken out into rhyme either . . . not yet.

After Mr. Harrington walked away, I looked back at Jono. "I feel like I've seen him somewhere before."

"You were at his house." A wrinkle formed between Jono's eyes.

"Come again?" When would I have been at that man's place?

"The fundraiser you went to last Friday. It was at Mr. Harrington's house."

Realization washed through me. "And his daughter is Misha."

"Yes, exactly."

I should have known that. But I had so many new people to keep track of. "Don't mind me. I'm still trying to remember all the new people I'm meeting here in town."

"It does take a while. He's a good one to get to know. He was a congressman for a few years. He also owns a tech company and the Oleander Resort."

The blood left my face. "The Oleander?"

That's where my father had worked when we'd moved back here.

"That's right. It's a great resort. You should go there sometime. Anyway, that invitation stands. If you would like to go with me to the golf tournament, I'd be honored."

"I'm afraid I'm not much of a golfer."

"You don't have to be. Then again, if you're interested in learning, I would be more than happy to teach you."

Why did I find myself playing with that idea for a moment? It seemed very unlike me. Yet, at the same time, the idea was intriguing. "Let me check my schedule then."

A big smile spread across his face.

Did I really want to dive this deeply into the wealthy in this town?

I wasn't sure.

For my father's sake, I would do whatever it took.

CHAPTER ELEVEN

JONO and I wrapped up our date. I was sad to say that he'd given no hints that he had known my father or knew about anything that had taken place in Yerba. That meant this date had pretty much been for nothing—except for the fact that I'd had a nice meal and it had gotten me back into the dating scene. But I wasn't sure if that was good or not. I was in no rush to find myself tangled up in romance and the drama that went with it.

Jono paid the bill and walked me outside. What was he going to think when he saw my car? I didn't know, and I didn't want to care.

But part of me did. I remembered Michael's words: *If he can't like you for who you are then does it really matter if he likes you at all?*

"Listen." Jono turned to me as we stood in the moonlight

on the sidewalk outside the restaurant. "You ever been on a yacht?"

"A yacht?" I repeated even though I'd clearly heard what he said.

A grin spread across his handsome face. "That's right. Mine is docked right over here. I thought you might want to hang out some more." He shrugged. "You know, in private."

All kinds of scenarios went through my head. None of them were worth repeating, but I knew that going on a boat with Jono right now wouldn't be in my best interest—on so many levels.

However, I still had questions to ask him—questions I hadn't been able to work into our conversation. Things like: Do you speak Spanish? Have you ever been to Yerba? Do you know anyone who works for the CIA?

"No, I can't," I started, making sure I sounded apologetic. "I need to get back home so I can get ready for work tomorrow."

He stared at me a minute, as if my answer genuinely surprised him. Finally, he nodded. "Okay then. I understand. But let me know about that golf tournament, okay?"

He obviously wasn't used to women telling him no. It was almost like he didn't know how to react.

"It's next month, correct?"

He nodded. "That's right."

"I'll see if it will work out, and I'll text you."

"That sounds good." Jono leaned forward and kissed my cheek.

A surprising shiver ran down my spine.

That was unexpected, but I couldn't read too much into it. There was so much more to attraction than bursts of warm fuzzy feelings.

"I look forward to hearing from you," he murmured.

With a wave, Jono turned to go back to his yacht, and I turned to go back to my beater.

The contrast wasn't lost on me. Jono and I were from two different worlds. I'd dated somebody who was from a different world than mine. Sergio. That hadn't worked out well.

It was a lesson I'd likely never forget.

As I walked back to my car, my thoughts raced. How was I going to find out what happened to my dad? I had absolutely no leads. Jono had been my best bet, and he had offered nothing.

The more I thought about it, the more I wondered if when I'd heard him say *mantente alerta* if I had totally misunderstood.

But how had my father died? Had it really been a heart attack or had that just been a cover-up?

It was too late now to ask for a reexamination of his body. Not without any proof, at least. It was too extreme. No one would take me seriously.

I was going to need to think about this and reexamine my options for the future.

Because if I wanted answers, I was going to need a better plan than the one I had now.

I froze when I reached my car.

My stomach sank as I stared at it.

All four of my tires were flat.

Someone had slashed them.

"SO YOU WERE EATING at Stockley's?" Detective Hunter asked, kneeling beside my car to examine my tires and take pictures.

"That's right." I crossed my arms, wishing I could just be at home right now. Wishing any other detective had come. Wishing my dad was still here to help me out in these situations.

"Were you alone?"

I felt the heat creeping up my neck. "No, I wasn't. I was meeting with a . . . a friend."

Hunter stood and locked his gaze with mine. "Does this friend have a name?"

"Jono." I coughed as I said his name.

"Could you repeat that?" The detective continued to look me in the eye, not bothering to hide his curiosity.

There was no need to delay this any longer. The detective

was going to get this information out of me, one way or another. I might as well make this as painless as possible. "Jono."

He raised an eyebrow. "You had dinner with Jono Harris?"

I nodded, trying to ignore the shock in his voice. Was I not pretty enough to be Jono's type? Maybe I didn't have enough curves or enough money or maybe even enough moxie. Whatever it was, I almost felt insulted—which was stupid.

I lifted my chin, defying my insecurity. "That's right."

"And did he walk you to your car?"

Something about the way Hunter said that made me think that he was judging both Jono and me. "No, he did not. We said goodbye right there on the sidewalk. He went back to his yacht, and I went to my car."

His eyebrows sank back down, and something close to surprise crossed his features. "I see. Have you touched anything?"

"Not even the car door."

"May I?" He held out his hand.

I handed him my keys, and he unlocked my door, opening it and peering inside.

He'd brought another officer with him, and that man was asking around at businesses to see if anyone had seen anything.

As Hunter examined the interior of my car, I glanced

down and saw something white on the ground. A piece of paper. I started to grab it but stopped myself.

"I know this might not be significant, but what's that?" I pointed at my find as a slight breeze fluttered the edges.

Hunter reached down and plucked up the paper with his gloved hand. Carefully, he opened it, and I watched as his eyes widened. He turned it toward me, and I read the words there.

Back off or else.

The words were written in a rough scrawl, like they'd been jotted quickly and maybe even carelessly.

But there was something else . . .

I leaned toward the paper and sniffed. "Do you mind?"

Hunter eyeballed me as if totally perplexed by my actions. "Just don't touch it."

I didn't plan on it. Instead, I leaned close and drew in a deep breath. The paper had a familiar smell. Where had I noticed that scent before?

"Keith Freddie . . ." I muttered.

"What?"

I shook my head, realizing I needed to make more sense. "I've smelled the odor on that paper before. It smells like the beer Keith Freddie drinks."

Hunter continued to stare at me, almost looking dumfounded. "Are you sure?"

I nodded, not a single doubt in my mind. "Of course."

"Other people could drink that beer too, of course. But, is there any reason why that man might do this to your tires?"

"Maybe because he did something to Trina and wants me to stop investigating." I waited for Hunter's reprimand.

Instead, he nodded slowly, still thoughtfully staring at me. "I see."

He said that a lot. His responses were so balanced that they made my head spin. I couldn't tell what he was really thinking. Maybe this guy should go into politics.

"We're going to have to get a tow truck for you. Is there a particular shop where you want this taken?"

I wasn't familiar with any of them. "Any recommendations?"

"Earl's is good."

"Then Earl's it is."

He pulled out his phone. "Very well then. Let me call them. Then I'll give you a ride home."

CHAPTER TWELVE

MY THOUGHTS RACED as I sat beside Hunter while he drove me to my house. I rattled off directions to him, and he seemed to know exactly where my neighborhood was.

"So, you're still trying to find Trina, aren't you?" he asked, almost sounding too casual.

And there it was. That was what he'd been wanting to say, wasn't it?

Would he try to dissuade me, until I would flee? Why couldn't he just let me be?

I shrugged, trying to push down my nerves. "I'm just asking around."

"In case no one has ever told you, asking questions can get people hurt."

"So I've seen." I rubbed my arms, remembering some of those incidents entirely too clearly.

"But you're not willing to let this drop?" He stole a glance at me.

How could I explain this to him? "I would want someone to do this for me if I was in their shoes. How could I possibly look the other way?"

"You've got a good heart, Elliot. I'll give you that. I just don't want to see you get caught in the crossfire."

I studied his perfect profile for a moment. Occasionally, the streetlight illuminated it, showing his straight nose and perfectly coifed hair. If only I could see his eyes, see what lingered in the depths there.

"I have a feeling you know more about Trina Morrison than you're letting on," I finally said.

He said nothing. For normal people, I would interpret that as agreeing. But with Hunter, I didn't know.

A few minutes of silence passed. I glanced at his vehicle and noticed how neat and clean it was—the interior looked the opposite of Michael's with his fast food wrappers and empty soda bottles.

It smelled good in here also, as if he'd wiped everything down with a leather-scented cleaner.

It fit everything I knew about Hunter.

"I have to admit," Hunter started. "I didn't see Jono as your type."

Why did people keep saying that? Should I be complimented or insulted?

"Who said he was my type? It's like I said, I was meeting a

friend for dinner."

"Generally, he doesn't have friends who are females."

"I can see he has quite the reputation here in town."

"Yes, he does. He thinks he's above the law. That's what money can do to people. Give them big heads."

"And I'm guessing you have a lot of people like that around here."

He twisted his head. "You can say that again."

We pulled up to the little bungalow that I called home. The little white house with a chain-link fence all the way around it, including the front yard. It wasn't much to look at, but it was a warm and safe place where my mom, sister, and I could stay. I couldn't complain about that.

"Here we are," Hunter said.

I hoped that my smile showed my gratitude. "Thank you so much for the ride. And I guess I should call Earl's in the morning about my car?"

"Hopefully, your insurance will cover this."

"I hope so. Because if it doesn't . . . it looks like I'm going to be walking for a while."

"Take care of yourself, Elliot."

I opened my door. "You too."

As I walked away, I couldn't help but feel a flush wash over me.

Dylan Hunter fascinated me. And I had no idea what to do about that.

"WHO WAS that who dropped you off?" My sister, Ruth, asked as soon as I walked in the door. She had obviously been waiting up for me. "And why do you smell like perfume and seafood?"

I pulled my shirt to my nose and took a sniff. She was right. I did smell like that.

"It's a long story," I said, slipping by her. "Where's Mama?"

I wasn't in the mood to explain why I'd gone out with someone I didn't really like and saw no future with.

Ruth crossed her thin arms, her light-brown hair falling over her shoulders. Looking at her, no one would guess she had a life-threatening disease. "Mama already went to bed. Apparently, she has a headache."

My heart panged as I heard my sister say those words. I knew my mom was having a hard time since my dad died. I wanted nothing more than to make things easier for her. But the more I worked to earn money for the family, the less time I had to spend at home. It was like a double-edged sword.

I set my purse on the table near the door, where all three of us left our things.

"So who drove you?" my sister persisted, staying on my heels.

"It was a detective, if you must know."

Her eyes widened. "A detective? What happened? Are you okay?"

I raised my hands. "I'm fine. But my tires got slashed. He had to give me a ride home."

The hopeful look in her gaze disappeared. "Oh. Is that all?"

"Were you hoping I got robbed instead?"

"No, of course not. I just was hoping that maybe you'd met somebody." As her words trailed off, a coughing fit seized her.

More worry coursed through me. She desperately needed that double lung transplant. How much longer would it be until it was her turn? And would we have the money when that turn happened?

"Ruth . . ." I reached for her.

She pushed me away and raised her hand. "I'm fine. It happens all the time."

"I know. And that's why I'm worried."

She straightened, and I knew she was trying to pull herself together, to look stronger. I would do the same thing in her shoes. "Enough about me. Why are you dressed like that? What were you doing when your tires got slashed?"

"If you must know, I was having dinner with somebody."

Her eyebrows shot up. "A guy?"

"Yes, a guy." I paused in the entryway in order to let the conversation play out.

"Who?"

"His name is Jono Harris."

Her eyes widened. "You went out on a date with Jono Harris?"

Great. What did she know about this man? It seemed like everybody knew about his reputation.

"Yes, I did. But it was just casual. I view it as a way of kind of getting me back into that scene."

"Good. It's time. I'm tired of seeing you moping about Sergio." She puckered her lips like she'd just eaten a lemon.

She knew about Sergio and me. She'd found me crying in my room and put the pieces together.

I tilted my head to the side and gave her a look. "Moping? I think you're exaggerating."

"Yes. That's exactly what you were doing. I can't blame you. I mean, the man did break your heart. He was a total jerk. But you were always too good for him anyway. And now that he's actually working for this new government leader who rose up in Yerba, that proves that he is scum."

I couldn't argue with her. I took a step toward my bedroom, suddenly feeling exhausted. But before I got there, I paused. I looked at my sister, realizing we hadn't had a good chance to talk all week. I worried about her—about all the changes in her life, about the new school she attended, about the new friends she hung out with.

"Is everything going okay with you?" I asked.

She nodded. "It is. I like the school. And I'm making some friends. So I can't complain."

"I'm glad to hear that, Ruth. I know this move has been hard on all of us."

"The only thing that's made it more bearable is having you and mom here with me." Ruth pulled me into a hug.

I held her close. I would do anything for my sister. Anything.

It was the whole reason I had taken this PI job, and knowing the importance of a sister was the reason I was helping Rebecca Morrison.

CHAPTER THIRTEEN

"SO HOW WAS your date with Jono?" Michael turned to me as we sat in his minivan outside of Nolan Burke's house the next morning.

I remembered last night's events.

This morning, when I'd called Earl's about my car, I'd discovered that my bill had already been paid. When I stepped outside, fully prepared to walk to the bus stop, my car was there with four new tires.

Hunter was the only person I could think of who would have done that. I tried to call him at the station—the only number I had—but he wasn't at work, as expected.

I was going to have to track him down and thank him later.

Right now, I was counting my blessings. Whoever had done this for me was a real lifesaver.

I looked back at Michael.

I had to admit that I had been dreading doing this stakeout again. I knew that not all detective work was exciting and glamorous, but this was just mind-numbing. And then, of course, Michael *had* to bring up my date.

"It was nice," I finally said, lowering my I-don't-feel-like-being-social novel. "Stockley's was a great restaurant, and it was a beautiful evening. I can't complain."

"Then, when it was over, Jono invited you back to his yacht, didn't he?"

My eyes widened. Had Michael been spying on me?

No, of course not. There was a more reasonable explanation.

"I guess it's a well-known fact that he does that," I said.

Michael twisted his head. "If I know about it, then I would definitely say yes."

"He did invite me onboard, as a matter of fact."

Michael studied my face before he finally asked, "Was his yacht as nice as people say it is?"

I crossed my arms, trying not to be offended—but I was. "Look, I know we haven't known each other for that long. But do you really think I would have gone to the yacht alone with him?"

He raised an eyebrow, a curious emotion dancing in his gaze. I couldn't identify it, though. Surprise? Satisfaction? Relief?

"So you didn't?" he clarified.

I didn't even offer a response. I just gave Michael a look that clearly stated I did not appreciate what he was considering.

"You're right, you're right." He leaned back, and his voice softened. "You don't seem the type who's going to fall for all of Jono's charms. It's just that, it surprised me that you even went out with him at all."

"I told you my reasons for it. How many times do we have to go over this?"

He almost seemed like he didn't hear me. "So are you going out with him again?"

"He invited me to a golf tournament next month. I'm thinking about it."

"Are you a golfer?"

I'd rather poke my eye out. "No, I'm not. But there are going to be a lot of people there, and I thought it would be a nice experiment in figuring out who's who in this town."

"I'm not sure you really want to know about all the people in this town." Michael readjusted his hat and stared off in the distance again.

I studied his face more. He'd made several statements like that, each of them cryptic and offering very few details. "You really don't like the people in this town, do you?"

He shrugged. "That's a long story."

"You always say that."

With a sigh, he picked up three of the oranges he'd

brought and began juggling. He liked to do that. I pictured him mentally sorting his thoughts at the same time.

"Maybe one day I'll tell you more," he finally said. "That's not something I usually talk about, however."

I glanced out the window. I wasn't going to push. I knew what it was like to need privacy. Instead, I leaned back and glanced at the little house Burke lived in. So far this morning, we hadn't seen him.

In the meantime, I was prepared to sort my mother's straight pins by size. She liked to sew, and the pile on her magnetic pincushion reminded me of a high-rise after an earthquake. I couldn't handle it any longer.

"How was Chloe's game last night?" I asked.

His countenance lifted at the mention. "It was great. Her team won so she was happy."

"She seems like a great girl."

A smile crossed his lips. "She is. Light of my life, hands down."

"Have you always coached her team for her?"

"Last year was my first year. I like it. Except politics try to work their way onto the field even at that age. It's the only thing I don't really like about being a coach."

"You don't seem like the type who lets people shove you around."

"I'm not. But it is annoying, to say the least."

I could understand that. I knew all about politics, even though the politics in Yerba were different than here in the

States. I would like to say things in my small South American country were somehow more wholesome than they were here.

But as I thought about how my country had basically imploded, I knew that they weren't.

Nothing was untouchable. Not countries. Not ideas. Not even relationships.

———————

JUST LIKE THE DAY BEFORE, Burke decided to go to the movies again. Maybe it was one of the few things he could do with his injuries. I didn't know, but it looked like Michael and I were done for the rest of the day.

Again.

He glanced at me. "What now?"

"You mean, you're not going back to the office?"

"I figured you probably wanted to continue investigating Trina."

He'd read my mind. "I would love to. I didn't think you'd want to, though."

"You need a supervisor." He gave me another look—part humored, part irritated, part I-like-giving-you-a-hard-time. "Now, where do you want to go?"

"I'm not going to get you in trouble, am I?"

"I put in a lot of after-hours work for Oscar. I think it will be fine. Besides, I'm just going to be a chauffeur. I warned you about taking on side cases, so my hands need to be clean here. I, for one, don't want to lose my job."

"Fine, you're just the chauffeur."

"So where are we headed, your Royal Yerbian Highness?"

"Careful or I might start to like hearing you talk like that," I said before adding, "Riverside."

"I had a feeling that's what you were going to say. But Riverside is a huge complex. How do you think you're going to find Trina there?"

"I'm not sure. But I hope to think of a way very soon."

Fifteen minutes later, we pulled up to a luxury condo complex located on the water about ten minutes north of Storm River. The whole area was immaculate and new.

I could only imagine what it cost to live at this place.

We found a parking space and walked toward the main entrance. Though it was a condo complex, Michael had told me that there was a front desk, an exercise center, and a meeting area for residents.

I smiled at the woman working behind the counter, trying to look approachable as I walked up to her. "Hi there. I'm hoping you can help me."

She looked up from her computer and raised an eyebrow on her thin, frowning face.

I could tell that she wasn't going to be the type who'd easily give answers. Something about her pinched features screamed prickly and uptight.

"What can I do for you? Do you live here?" Wrinkles

formed around her lips as she puckered them, waiting for my answer.

"Actually, I don't, but a friend of mine does. I'm supposed to meet her, but I can't remember which condo she lives in."

Her eyebrows climbed higher, and her lips puckered even tighter before she said, "Did you try to call her?"

Her haughty tone put me on edge. "I did, but my friend's one of those who always lets her phone die. She's not answering. In the meantime, I just drove two hours so we could catch up. Is there any way you could help me out?"

Lying came a little too easily for me, and that fact left me feeling off-balance. I'd been struggling with that realization ever since I took this job, and I was still learning how to cope.

Certainly, God saw through my desperate attempts for forgiveness as I prayed that He would understand my reasons for fibbing.

"I don't know what to say," the woman said. "Privacy and all. I'm not allowed to tell you where our residents live."

"Even if that resident is a friend?" I smiled sweetly—that *was* something I was good at doing. *Make your weakness into strengths.*

My dad had written that in his journal.

"Since there's no way for me to prove that, then the answer is no."

My sweetness had failed.

"I see. I understand, and I wouldn't want for you to do

anything that makes you uncomfortable. I just don't know what else I can do to get in contact with her."

"Maybe her phone will charge soon." What clearly sounded like annoyance filled her voice before she turned back to her computer, indicating our conversation was done.

I glanced at Michael. Maybe I should have come up with another plan. But I don't know what that plan might have been. This woman was tight-lipped, and it didn't seem to matter what kind of cover story I concocted. She probably wouldn't have budged. Stubbornness seemed to be etched into the fine lines of her face.

Michael took my elbow and led me away. When we stepped outside, he turned to me. "It was a good try."

At least he hadn't said, "I told you so."

"Is there any other way we might be able to find her here?" I asked.

"Not if we don't know where she's staying. This place is big."

Someone paused beside us, a man who'd been walking toward the front door with some workout clothes on. "Maybe I can help. You're looking for someone? I didn't mean to eavesdrop. I know this complex can get confusing sometimes."

My pulse spiked. "That would be great if you could. Her name is Trina Morrison. Do you know her?"

"Trina?" The man's face lost some of its friendliness.

"Yeah, I know Trina. She's in 241. Take a left around the corner, go to the next building, and you'll see it."

"Thank you so much," I gushed.

"We met a few times." The man shrugged. "You two seem way too nice to have a friend like her. But have fun catching up."

Before we could talk any more, the man slipped inside.

I wasn't complaining, however.

Now I just needed to find the condo with the numbers 241.

CHAPTER FOURTEEN

AS MICHAEL and I stood outside Trina's condo, I raised my hand to knock, but Michael pulled my fist down before I could.

"What are you going to do if she's here?" He propped an arm on the door and leaned into it, effectively stopping me in my tracks.

As I stared at his bicep, I felt my throat grow dry. That wasn't my normal reaction. I wasn't an I-love-muscles type of girl. But the look was good on Michael.

I rubbed my throat and looked away. "Then I am going to tell her that her sister is looking for her."

"And if she doesn't care?"

"Then I'll have to deal with that when I know. What else can I do?"

He leaned closer and lowered his voice. "I just want you

to be prepared that things may not go the way you think they will. Provided that Trina is home, of course. If she's not, none of this will be an issue, obviously."

"Well, let's just see what happens." I remembered more of my dad's advice. *Make your roadblocks hurdles instead.* That's exactly what I planned on doing.

I knocked and waited.

Nothing.

I knocked again. And, again, there was no answer.

Did we come all this way for nothing? That's how it appeared. I'd badly wanted to find answers today, both on the Burke case and on this one. I was supposed to meet with Rebecca tonight to give her an update, and I'd been hoping for good news.

"It was a nice try," Michael said. "You could always come back again later."

I nodded, trying to hide my disappointment. "I know. But I'm not quite done yet."

"What do you mean?" He turned his head, his eyes narrowed with anticipation.

"My father used to say that persistence was my finest quality as well as my worst." That said, I walked to the condo next door and knocked on it as well.

I waited, hoping that somebody might answer. To my delight, an older woman cracked the door open.

"Can I help you?" She observed us with her one visible eye.

I plastered on my friendliest smile. "I'm hoping you can. I'm looking for my friend Trina next door. Have you, by chance, seen her lately?"

"No, I actually haven't seen her for more than a week. Sorry I can't be more help." She started to shut her door.

I couldn't let that happen. "Wait! I know this is going to sound strange, but I've traveled quite a way to see her. Do you know where else I might be able to find her?"

The woman's lips twitched for a moment, and I realized she was probably contemplating closing the door on me anyway. I held my breath, waiting to see what she was going to do.

The door closed.

But my hopes lifted when I heard the chain drop and then saw the door reopen, fully this time. A petite woman with lovely white hair, probably in her seventies, stared at us.

I let out a breath of relief.

"Sorry about that, but you can never be too careful," the woman said. "Now, about your question. I only talked to Trina a couple of times. She hasn't lived here long. But during one of our conversations she said something about working for Elite Event Services."

"What's that?" I asked.

"They're event planners, from what Trina told me. Their offices are located somewhere in Storm River. I would try there."

"I'll do that," I said before remembering Michael's advice

during our last case. Before she closed the door, I added, "Is there anything else about Trina that stands out to you? Anything strange that happened?"

The woman's gaze darkened. "Honestly, I'm glad to see her gone. She was the kind who thought of no one but herself. Good luck."

Ouch. "Thanks so much for your help."

The woman nodded and slipped back into her condo.

When she was gone, I looked up at Michael, hoping he might be a little proud of me. "It looks like I have somewhere else to keep looking, at least."

"It looks like you do." He nudged my shoulder with his fist. "Good job, Champ."

"Champ?" I was still getting familiar with all of the American expressions.

"Yeah, you know, like somebody who wins at sporting events. Anyway, I have to admit that your persistence is paying off."

"That's good, at least." As I said the words, I turned and looked around.

There was that feeling again.

The feeling I was being watched.

I didn't see anyone nearby. To the visible eye, there was nothing that should cause this feeling—except maybe paranoia.

The water was behind us. More condos on either side. A small grassy area just below.

As a boat sped past, the two people on deck didn't even look our way.

There was nothing else.

So what was causing this reaction in me?

"What is it?" Michael squinted.

My gaze went back to him, and I studied his face, looking for a sign of the truth. "You don't sense it?"

Michael narrowed his eyes as he continued to stare at me. "Sense what?"

I shook my head, realizing how crazy I was going to sound. "Never mind."

As I started to take a step, Michael grabbed my arm and his gaze latched onto mine. "No, really. I want to know. What do you sense right now?"

I paused and released a pent-up breath. Did I really want to go there? I would be opening . . . what was that American expression? A can of . . . something. Caterpillars?

That fit the mental image I'd stored away, though I couldn't fathom the origin of the phrase.

"Like someone's watching us," I finally said. "But I don't see anybody."

Michael's gaze scanned everything around us before landing on me again. "How long have you felt this way?"

"You really want to know?"

"Of course. I wouldn't have asked otherwise."

I rubbed my lips together before saying, "About ten days."

"You've been feeling like somebody has been watching

you for ten days?" Michael's voice rose with surprise. "And this is the first time you've mentioned it? Elliot . . ."

I shrugged, wanting to believe he was overreacting. "I want to believe that I can trust my instincts, but I've seen no proof. Except for the night that the shadow followed me home."

"The shadow followed you home?" Michael stared at me like I'd lost my mind.

Since I'd opened that door, I guess I was going to have to explain. "It was one of the nights my car broke down, and I'd been working late. As I was walking home, I heard footsteps behind me. I didn't see anybody, but I'm sure someone was there."

Michael stared at me in disbelief. "I can't believe you didn't mention this earlier."

I shrugged again, my level of worry rising exponentially. "There was no proof of anything or even any good reason to explain it."

The only reason I could think of was that it had to do with my father's death. But I couldn't tell Michael that. If I did, we'd be here for a while. Plus, there were other implications of sharing the information. My dad being a spy had upped the stakes.

"Last night, someone slashed my tires while I was at the restaurant," I admitted with a touch of hesitance.

"What?" His voice rose.

"I filed a police report," I insisted. "I followed all the rules."

"You have no idea who did it?"

"No idea."

Michael surveyed everything around us one more time. "I don't see anybody watching us right now, Elliot."

"I know. That's why I should have never said anything." I tapped his shoulder with my fist. "*Champ.*"

He let out a chuckle but it quickly faded. "You know if you ever need me, you can call me whenever you need, right? Slashed tires and being followed are no joke. If you're in some kind of trouble . . ."

The sincerity in his voice filled me with warmth. I smiled up at him, gratitude filling me. "I appreciate that, Michael. Thank you. I don't know that I'm in trouble. Maybe I just have bad luck."

We all needed someone to watch out for us.

But he also had a daughter to watch out for. I knew I wouldn't be able to live with myself if I ever did anything that put either of them in danger.

Which was another reason why I couldn't tell him about my father.

MICHAEL and I returned to the office for a little while, gave

Oscar the update on the case, and then I had just enough time to run to The Board Room to meet with Rebecca.

Unlike last time, today she was already seated at a table and drinking a soda when I walked in. Her eyes lit with recognition when she spotted me.

"Elliot." She stood, her voice thin and her motions fast, almost jittery. "I've been so anxious about this meeting."

I sat across from her, and she followed suit. "Anxious?"

Her hands hugged the soda in front of her. "I've just been anxious to know what you learned. I just know you're going to find her."

I really needed to lower her expectations.

"I've been making some good progress." I told her about everything that I had done so far, in between ordering my cheese and cracker board.

"So you haven't found her?" Rebecca's lips drooped in disappointment and her shoulders slumped. "With every minute that passes, I worry that she's in pain or suffering. I almost can't handle it."

Despite everything I had told her, she was obviously not impressed.

But I understood her concern.

"Like I said, I found where Trina was living, and I know where she's been working. Tomorrow, I'm going to follow up and see what else I can learn."

She frowned, still looking disappointed. "I guess that will have to do then. I do wish you had more."

I bit back a retort. I really wanted to remind Rebecca that I was doing this out of goodwill, and I wasn't charging anything. The least she could do was to show some gratitude.

But I bit back those words, knowing that it might be trauma and grief talking instead of Rebecca in her normal state. Yet the old saying, *no good deed goes unpunished* echoed in my mind. I hoped I didn't regret stepping in to help her.

"I thought of one other thing," she said, pushing her drink aside.

I leaned toward her, anxious to hear what she had to say. "What's that?"

"The last time I saw my sister, she was wearing a lot of new jewelry. She said it was a gift from somebody."

"She never said who?"

"She didn't. But I had the impression he was someone powerful. Someone with money."

Keith had said something similar. "I'll see if I can find out anything."

"She also accidentally called me a couple weeks ago," Rebecca continued. "Later, she changed her phone number. Anyway, I couldn't make out everything she was saying, but I heard her say something about an exciting investment opportunity at Mac—"

"Mac what?"

Rebecca shrugged. "I have no idea. It cut off before I could hear the rest. I would have mentioned it earlier, but little bits and pieces keep coming back to me. I'm sorry. It's a lot to comprehend."

"I understand. I'll see if that can somehow help me in some way. Thank you."

"I really need to know what happened to her." Rebecca grabbed my hand, and her gaze pierced into me. "I don't think that my life will ever be the same until I know."

I knew what that was like. I didn't think I would ever be able to truly relax until I knew what happened to my father. But, just like Rebecca, I was at a dead end. Actually, Rebecca had way more leads in her case than I had in mine. All I had was a theory—I had no suspects, no motives, no clues even.

"I'm doing my best," I told her. "You just have to trust me on that one."

"I know. It's just so hard."

"There's something else I need to tell you, Rebecca," I continued. "Someone slashed my tires last night."

She sucked in a breath. "What? Was it because of this investigation?"

"I don't know."

She shook her head and leaned back. "You know what? Maybe you shouldn't do this. Maybe it's too dangerous."

"I'll be careful."

She assessed me with her gaze. "I don't want anyone getting hurt . . ."

I reached across the table and squeezed her arm. "I'll be careful. I promise."

Finally, she nodded and her hope-filled eyes met mine. "You'll keep me updated?"

"I will."

She smiled and stood, dropping a couple bills on the table. "Great. I'll be seeing you around then. But I've got to get to work now."

Well, this had been an unfruitful meeting. Maybe it was just as well. I could go home and spend some time with my mom and sister. But my sister had been all about her friends lately, and my mom had been working extra shifts. She'd made some new friends at church also, and she'd been spending some free time with them. I knew the social interaction was good for her.

But the last thing I wanted to do was to go home and just sit by myself.

As I wandered back outside, I paused and looked back at the harbor area. I remembered my date with Jono last night. Part of me wouldn't be surprised if I saw him pull up here again right now, another date in tow. It was a good thing I didn't have a major crush on the guy or I might be really disappointed.

Out of curiosity, I wandered down to the docks and walked up and down the wooden planks there. Boats that cost ten times as much as our house were docked in the water. They were beauties.

"Fancy seeing you here," someone said.

My back muscles tightened as I turned around, not

knowing whom to expect. To my surprise, Detective Hunter stood there, leaning casually against a wooden post. He was dressed in jeans, a T-shirt, and boat shoes.

The look was nice on him.

"Nor was I expecting to see you here." I stepped toward him and paused. "You following me?"

He chuckled and shook his head. "No, I'm just hanging out."

"Just hanging out?"

He shrugged. "I'm actually fixing up a boat here in my free time."

"Sounds nice."

"It will be. It will let me do a little fishing. Nothing like eating a dinner you caught yourself."

"I agree." I missed freshly caught fish and fruit picked from my backyard. Maybe one day, when I had more time on my hands, I could plant a garden and live off the land more.

But right now, I was just grateful for a paycheck.

"How about you?" He joined me as I ambled down the dock. "What brings you this way?"

"I just met with somebody at The Board Room. I'm about to head back home now."

"Jono?"

I let out a quick laugh. "No."

He nodded and walked with me back toward the parking lot. "I was overstepping. It's not my business."

"It's okay. By the way, thank you for my tires."

"Your tires?"

I tried to read his expression. Was he pretending not to know? I wasn't sure.

"You paid to have them fixed and then brought my car back to my house," I explained to him.

"Did I?"

I still couldn't read him. "Didn't you?"

"I don't know what you're talking about." His expression showed nothing.

But I still knew it had to be him. "Well, thank you. It was such an incredible blessing to me."

He glanced at me, still not acknowledging he'd had any part of it. "That's great that you had a car to drive this morning."

Wait . . . had he really not done it?

I still wasn't sure. Before I could interrogate him more, he changed the subject.

"You know, I've been thinking a lot about that conversation we had over coffee a couple days ago," Hunter said.

"Oh yeah?" I had no idea where he was going with this. Another lecture? Had he thought of more reasons I shouldn't be doing this job?

"There's something I'd like to show you."

My eyebrows shot up. "Is that right? Does it have to do with the Beltway Killer?"

He chuckled, his eyes dancing. He seemed like a different person when he was off duty.

"No, it doesn't," he said. "But I think you'll like it. If you think you can trust me enough to take a little trip."

I wished I could say yes without reservation. Then I remembered the fact that somebody was following me, and the fact that I wasn't sure whom I could trust.

But this man was a detective. Certainly, he was noble, right?

Then again, I had worked with politicians in Yerba. They were supposed to be trustworthy and look out for the best interests of the public.

They'd ended up being full of corruption.

You couldn't let someone's career determine if they were someone you could trust or not. But as I stood in front of Hunter now, I really wanted to trust him. Besides, I didn't want to go home and sit by myself.

Finally, I shrugged. "Sure. I'm up for something new."

A slow smile spread across his face. "Great. Can you go now?"

"Why not?"

I hoped I didn't regret this. But an even greater part of me just felt excited.

CHAPTER FIFTEEN

A FEW MINUTES LATER, I was riding down the road in Detective Hunter's pickup truck. Just as I'd expected, the inside was pristine. Everything about the man was nice and neat. Even his hair always looked perfectly balanced, as did his features.

Darkness filled the space outside, adding a little more mystery to this whole outing. I wasn't sure if that was a good or bad thing.

"So how's your investigation going?" Hunter slipped a piece of spearmint gum into his mouth before offering me a piece.

I politely declined.

"It's going," I said, unsure how much I should reveal about my life and investigations. I had to be a smart girl here and not one given to impulses.

"You haven't gotten yourself into any more trouble, have you?" He stole a glance at me.

"Nope. I'm proud to report that I've had a couple of trouble-free days." I chose to stay quiet about the fact of being watched. No need to open up that can of caterpillars.

"That's good news." He glanced at me in all of his Captain America glory. "Did you find Trina?"

"Not yet. But I found out where she was working, so I'm hoping her coworkers might have some answers."

"Good luck with your case."

I couldn't tell if he was sincere or not, so I decided to move on.

"Are you from around this area?" I asked him, realizing I really didn't know much about the man other than the fact that he was handsome.

"I'm actually from Georgia."

"Georgia?" That explained the gentle, rolling Southern accent. I had cousins who lived down there. "How'd you end up here, if you don't mind me asking?"

His smile slipped a little. "My fiancée went to college up near DC and then she got accepted into a doctorate program afterward. I moved up here to be with her."

I remembered the article I had seen about the Beltway Killer. Then I remembered seeing a picture of a woman he'd had on his desk. It was the same woman who'd been listed as a victim. But I wasn't supposed to know that, so I wasn't even sure how much I could say.

"Your fiancée, huh?" That seemed lackluster but safe enough.

"She died a year ago." He rubbed his throat as the words left his lips. He didn't have to tell me for me to know that his heart still ached with loss.

"I'm sorry to hear that." And I was. I knew all about grief and how horrible it was. I wouldn't wish it upon my greatest enemy.

"Me too." His voice took on a raspy tone. "We were supposed to get married last month."

If Sergio and I had still been together, that's when we'd talked about also—provided we didn't elope. Instead, he'd ghosted me, as Michael had explained. "That's awful. How long were the two of you together?"

"Five years."

"Five years? That's a long time." Sergio and I had only dated six months. I suddenly felt like I had no right to be heartbroken.

"She was finishing her doctorate in psychology."

"What was her name?" I'd seen it in a news article I read, but I wanted to let him talk about her.

"Kate."

"I guess you decided to stay here anyway?" I leaned back in the seat, settling in for our conversation.

"That's right. The area is interesting. I don't know how long I'll be here. But for a while."

"I was engaged also before I moved here from Yerba," I

offered. As soon as the words left my lips, I wondered what I was thinking. Was I opening up to this man?

It wasn't my smartest move. But I missed having community. The worst part about leaving Yerba was the loneliness I now felt. Still, I needed to be wise.

Hunter glanced at me as he headed down the road. "Were you?"

"I was. But I just have to remind myself that everything works out as it's supposed to in matters of the heart like this."

I shifted, and my foot skimmed something on the floor. A business card that had fallen beneath the floormat.

I glanced at it, trying to read the words there as flashes of light filled the space every time we passed a streetlamp.

Peru.

Peruvian.

With each flash, more of the words came into focus.

Peruvian embass—

Peruvian embassy.

My heart raced. This was the business card for the ambassador from Peru, I realized.

Peru was Yerba's sister country and shared a border.

Why in the world would Hunter be in contact with the ambassador from Peru? The country was trying to offer diplomatic resources to help the Yerbian people. Many had tried to take refuge there.

What if there was more to Detective Hunter than I ever imagined?

I decided not to say anything to Hunter about it. Not now. Not while I was alone.

Hunter slowed before pulling down a dark drive. "Here we are."

I glanced around, suddenly second-guessing myself again. He'd taken me to somewhere in the middle of nowhere, it was getting dark, and no one knew I was with him.

Suddenly, this seemed like a very bad idea.

What if Hunter was secretly the enemy?

And what if this had all been a trap?

CHAPTER SIXTEEN

HUNTER KEPT DRIVING down the dark lane until he stopped near a two-story house. My nerves still felt frazzled as he shifted his truck into Park. I had no idea why he had brought me here. But I could see bad things happening.

Things like dying under mysterious circumstances like my father. Being tortured for answers I didn't have. Being left abandoned on the side of the road with no one around to hear my cries for help.

"This will make sense in a minute," Hunter explained, glancing over at me with a smile.

Would it all make sense because I was going to end up dead? I tried to shake the thought, but I couldn't.

He climbed out, walked around to my side, and opened my door for me. I felt a slight tremble rush through me as he took my arm to help me out.

"Close your eyes," he instructed.

Was that so I wouldn't see the gun he pulled?

Another thought dropped into my mind with enough weight to make me flinch.

What if Hunter was the Beltway Killer? Was that why he didn't want me to investigate the case? Had he killed his own fiancée?

The questions kept hitting me like machine-gun fire. I was letting fear get the best of me, but I felt helpless to stop it.

I closed my eyes. If Hunter was going to kill me, having my eyes opened or closed wasn't going to change a thing. But I really should have told someone where I was going. If I'd thought about it earlier, at least I could have texted Michael so he'd know where to look for me when it came time to find my dead body.

With a hand still grasping my elbow, Hunter led me away from the truck. I peeked my eyes open just enough to see he was leading me behind the dark, almost deserted-looking house.

"I think you're going to like this. I've been thinking about it ever since we talked at the coffee shop."

Had he been thinking about killing me ever since then? I did fit the profile of the Beltway Killer's victims. I was going to have to start being more careful.

If I even got that opportunity again.

A strange sound hit my ears. Sure, we were surrounded

by woods right now. All the normal sounds of nature filled the air. The rustle of leaves as the breeze blew. The scampering of nighttime critters. Somewhere in the distance, a dog barked.

But none of those things were what begged for my attention.

No, it was a different sound, a sound I hadn't heard in a long time.

I wanted to peek, but almost as if the detective knew what I was thinking, he put a hand over my eyes, not allowing me to.

As he did, his piney cologne filled my senses. It really was a nice scent.

Why did the killer have to be someone so handsome who seemed so nice? Why couldn't he be ugly and vicious looking? And why wasn't I fighting back? My dad taught me some self-defense moves. They might buy me a little time. Then I could run into the woods and—

Before I could finish that thought, I heard metal on metal. One of Hunter's hands released me. He seemed to be fidgeting with something.

Was he putting me in a cage? Would I be on the other end of his rage? Maybe this man was tricky because this situation felt so life-threatening and sticky.

My thoughts kept going to darker and darker places.

That did it. I needed to fight back. There was no way I could go inside to wherever he was leading me.

But then, Hunter dropped his hand and nudged me forward. "Open your eyes. This is it."

I pulled my eyes open, bracing myself for the worst.

Torture chambers. Makeshift prisons. A doctor holding a needle.

Yeah, that was a big fear of mine.

Instead, the air left my lungs as Hunter flipped a soft light on.

Probably fifty birds of all types surrounded me. Tropical birds. Birds like the ones I had woken up to in Yerba every morning. Macaws. Parrots. Parakeets.

Branches and fountains had been set up and the birds happily flew from one perch to another.

"This is . . . wonderful," I whispered, turning in a circle and soaking in every glorious detail.

Hunter grinned softly beside me. "I thought you would like it."

I turned to face him, questions filling me. "Where *are* we?"

"A friend of mine likes to rehabilitate birds. He eventually had so many that he set up this sanctuary for them. He keeps it climate-controlled so the birds feel right at home, no matter the season."

I turned around again, unable to believe my eyes. "I love it."

"Does it remind you of home?"

Warmth rushed through me, and I closed my eyes. In an

instant, I was transported back in time. Back to a place where I felt happy. When my family was whole. When I had no idea what the future held.

I remembered hearing the birds singing as I awoke in the morning. I could even smell the briny scent of jungle air and hear the leaves from rainforest trees brushing each other with the breeze.

"It definitely reminds me of home," I murmured.

He smiled again. "Good. Because we all deserve to be reminded of home every once in a while."

I FELT MORE content than I had in months as Hunter and I drove away from the bird sanctuary. Who would have ever thought that today would have turned out like it did? And who would have ever thought that Hunter would have something to do with it?

A comfortable silence fell between us as we headed down the road back to my vehicle. I temporarily forgot about the business card I'd seen on the floor. Maybe he had a good reason to have the ambassador's contact information, something totally unrelated to me.

"So, are you still working for Oscar?" Hunter asked.

I wondered how long he'd been waiting to ask that question.

There was some type of history between Oscar and

Hunter, but I didn't know what. Oscar didn't want to talk about it, and I hated to ruin the evening by asking Hunter.

"I am," I finally said.

"You're a better person than I am to be able to purposefully work for him for that long." A certain edge of bitterness crept into Hunter's voice.

I decided to try to keep the conversation in safe territory. "It's been a pretty lame assignment this week. A workers' comp claim. We've just been watching this guy, waiting for him to mess up for three days, but it feels like three years."

"Yeah, that doesn't sound like very much fun. But that's the way it has to work sometimes, isn't it? Patience can lead to answers. So much of detective work isn't fun or glamorous."

"You're right. I'm still learning the ropes."

"What did you do back in Yerba?"

"I worked for one of the province legislators. I was his chief of staff."

Hunter quickly glanced my way. "Was he part of the corruption that was going on there?"

I held back a frown. "I didn't know it at the time, but, yes, he was. He sided with the leader of the philanthropic party —that's what they called it, but they were anything but generous. The leader of that party eventually overthrew our government. My family and I were lucky to get out when we did. Thankfully, my mom is American, and we had dual citizenship."

Even as I said the words, I wondered how much Hunter really knew. The man was tightlipped. And he had some kind of Peruvian connection.

So many questions raced through my head.

I desperately wanted to believe I could trust him, but I couldn't be stupid.

"Why'd you come to Storm River?" he asked.

"My family wanted to be close to DC because that's where the best doctor for my sister is. She has cystic fibrosis."

"But Storm River?"

"My dad had a contact in this area who's letting us rent our house for relatively cheap. It seemed like a win. But my dad died two months ago." My voice caught as I said the words.

"I'm sorry to hear that. What happened, if you don't mind me asking?"

"He had a heart attack. Out of the blue. Seemed healthy, but I have to wonder if some of the stress got to him. Not only was there the danger in the country when we left, but he was in the middle of trying to figure out how to get us out and how to get my sister the medical care she needed. Then once we came here, he had to find a job. He went from . . . working for the government to working maintenance for a resort in town. It was a big change."

"I can only imagine."

We pulled into the parking area, and he put his truck into Park. "Well, Elliot Ransom. It was nice hanging out with you for a while. You're not like most of the people here in town."

I wasn't sure if he considered that a good or a bad thing, but I wasn't going to ask.

"Thank you for giving me a taste of home," I said instead. "I appreciate it."

Our gazes caught for a minute, and we exchanged smiles.

"Stay safe," Hunter said.

I nodded to him as I climbed from the truck. "You too."

CHAPTER SEVENTEEN

I WAS STILL GRINNING as I climbed into my car, and I took off down the road for home.

Detective Hunter had surprised me. And having a taste of home had felt good—much better than I had even imagined.

But as headlights glared in my rearview mirror, I squinted.

Why was someone driving so closely?

I pressed on my brakes, trying to indicate for the driver to slow down.

It didn't seem to work.

The vehicle crept even closer. And, based on the height of the headlights, it was a big vehicle. Maybe even a truck.

What in the world was this guy doing? Had he had too much to drink?

As soon as I saw a place where I could pull off and let him pass, I would do that.

But before I could even look at my options, I felt a bump.

I lurched forward.

This guy had hit me.

This wasn't an accident.

This guy was coming after me, I realized.

My heart throbbed into my ears. What was going on here? Was this the same person who'd slashed my tires and left me that note, warning me off this case?

That was the only thing that made sense. Someone was desperate for me to leave Trina Morrison's disappearance alone.

That could only mean one thing.

That I was getting too close to answers.

But none of that would mean anything if I didn't survive this trip home.

I glanced around me. Little houses lined the side of the street. If I wasn't careful, my car was going to end up running into one of them. I couldn't let that happen.

I glanced in my rearview mirror again.

The vehicle revved up to hit me again.

I had to do something.

I wished I could call Hunter, but this car didn't have Bluetooth, and I couldn't risk grabbing my phone.

That meant I was on my own.

I glanced at the street ahead of me, desperate to find some way out of this situation.

I saw nothing.

As I came upon an intersection, I jerked my steering wheel to the right as hard as I could. My tires squealed as they skidded across the road.

But I made the turn.

I glanced behind me. The truck behind me had also made the turn.

Rats!

Where could I go right now? I didn't want to go somewhere where I would be alone with this lunatic. But I didn't want to put anyone in danger either.

I needed to think, and I needed to think quickly.

There was a park up ahead. If I could make it there, maybe I could somehow lose this guy. Or, if he did hit me, nobody else would be in danger.

I made a sharp left and the park came into view.

Just as I reached it, the truck rammed my bumper and my car began to spin.

I closed my eyes, having no idea what might happen next. But I prayed I would survive it.

MY CAR MAY HAVE STOPPED spinning, but not my head. Everything around me still seemed to be in motion.

Finally, my vision cleared. For a moment, at least.

I saw the truck speeding away into the distance.

As it did, my breath caught.

I'd seen that truck somewhere before.

And I knew exactly where.

Keith Freddie had a picture of himself beside that vehicle inside his apartment.

He was the one who had done this.

My hands shook as I pulled my car door open. I climbed out and looked around.

Miraculously, I hadn't hit anything. But I still wasn't sure I was in the right frame of mind to drive home.

Instead, I climbed back into my car and nearly collapsed there.

That had been close. A little *too* close for my comfort.

I needed to call Hunter and tell him about Keith Freddie's truck. It seemed like something he would need to know, whether or not he thought Trina Morrison's case was important.

So much for my good day.

CHAPTER EIGHTEEN

I HAD permission to go into work late the next day. I hadn't wanted to ask, but Elite Event's hours for the day were listed as from eight to three. If I waited until after work, they'd be closed, and I didn't want to waste any more time.

Surprisingly, Oscar hadn't asked too many questions, but I *had* started our conversation by reminding him about some of the overtime I'd done for him recently.

It was a risky move for someone who'd only worked at the place for just over a week, but I'd decided to take the chance.

Oscar seemed relatively understanding, but he made me promise to bring him some girly sounding coffee with toffee and whipped cream on top tomorrow morning in return for the favor.

Instead, I headed to Elite Events to see what I could find

out about Trina. The good news was that nothing had indicated that Trina was dead or that she had been captured by
the Beltway Killer.

I *had* discovered her new residence and her new place of
employment. I was still hoping for more answers, still hoping
that maybe Trina was just a jerk and that was the reason she
wasn't answering her sister's calls. But I needed to know for
sure before I moved on.

For Rebecca's sake.

As I pulled up to the storefront and put my car into Park,
my phone rang.

I recognized Hunter's number.

I'd called him at the police station last night to let him
know that someone had run me off the road, but I was okay.
He'd come out to take pictures of the tire prints and to ask
around if anyone had seen anything.

"I just wanted to let you know that Keith Freddie said his
truck was stolen yesterday morning," Hunter announced.

"And you believe him?" I gripped my phone, feeling a
touch of outrage. Couldn't that just be an excuse?

"We're still looking into it. I just wanted to give you that
update. Be careful out there today. Until we know what's
going on, you could be in danger. It appears someone is
targeting you."

"I noticed," I muttered as I stared out my window at the
sign reading, "Elite Events." The gold color and fancy font
seemed to signify royalty.

"I'm serious, Elliot," Hunter said. "I don't want to see you get hurt. Someone was willing to run you off the road to get you off the case. That's serious."

I knew better than to argue. Instead, I thanked Hunter, ended the call, and climbed from my car. As I headed toward the sidewalk, my hubcap fell off and clattered to the ground. I glanced around to see if anyone had seen but saw no watching eyes.

Quickly, I tried to shove it back on, but the disc wouldn't stay in place. Instead, I tossed the hubcap on my back seat.

I would have to worry about that at another time.

Instead, I brushed my hair back from my shoulders and squared my chin. I needed to tap into the meddling part of myself, for better or for worse.

I stepped inside Elite Events.

Even though the business was officially located in Storm River, it wasn't in the prime retail district. It was situated on the edge of town. But the building was nice, and it looked both updated and well maintained.

The sign up on top was slightly crooked, which probably bothered only me. For that matter, probably nobody else would notice that the left side was slightly lower than the right. Had people ever heard of a level? Best. Tool. Ever.

But I had other things to worry about at the moment.

I tugged at the door and was pleasantly surprised to find it was unlocked. Part of me feared that, even though the website said it opened at eight a.m., it wouldn't.

A woman with short brown hair, a simple white shirt, and a classic pearl necklace sat at the front desk.

"Hello there," she practically purred. "How can I help you?"

"Hi there," I started. "I am trying to find someone. I met her a couple weeks ago, and I believe she works here. It's about an upcoming event."

"And who would that be?" Her voice was the epitome of professional.

"Her name is Trina."

I watched the woman's face carefully, trying to read her expression as soon as she heard the name. But her face and expression remained placid.

"Trina did work for us. But she stopped showing up about two weeks ago." Her words remained crisp and unaffected.

"That's too bad. She seemed really great, and I was hoping to talk to her."

"Well, you're going to have to find someone else to talk to you, I'm afraid. She's no longer here, and I can't tell you how to get in touch with her." The frown she offered was too fast to seem sincere.

"Is there anybody above you I might be able to talk to, by chance? It's really important that I find her. We discussed an idea that I really think is proprietary."

The receptionist's expression remained unchanged.

"Jenna is in charge of the company. But she's busy. In fact, I doubt she'll have time to talk to you."

Ever so subtly, the woman glanced down at my jeans, T-shirt, and Converse. It was clear with that one look that she didn't approve. It was almost like she could sniff out potential clients who were too poor to afford their services. Quite the talent.

"Could you at least ask her?" I blinked, trying to look hard to resist.

The woman stared at me another moment before wheeling her chair across the floor and knocking at a frosted glass door behind her. "Jenna, you have someone here to see you."

"What do they want?" a voice called from the other side.

"It's about Trina."

"Don't know anything about her. Tell whoever it is to go away."

So much for this place being more sophisticated than Oscar's. I felt like I'd seen a crack in the façade, that I'd been given a glimpse behind the curtain.

The receptionist turned back to me and offered a mockingly regretful smile. "You heard it yourself. She doesn't have time."

There was one more approach I was toying with in the back of my mind. I didn't want to use it—but it looked like I was going to have to.

"Let me level with you," I started, leaning a hand on the

fake marble covering her desk. "Have you ever heard of Oscar Driscoll?"

Her lips curled in a half smile and curiosity lit her eyes. "He's the PI, right? He's been all over TV. Even had that movie about him and that case he solved."

I nodded. "I work for him. We're looking into Trina's disappearance. If it turns out there's a big story on her disappearance, you guys could play a big role in helping crack our case. You know that Hollywood's always pursuing Oscar, trying to hear about his new cases so they can make another blockbuster movie. They've even approached him about having his own talk show."

As soon as the words left my lips, I was certain that it wasn't going to work. The ploy sounded ludicrous, even to my own ears. Not to mention that the words weren't even the truth. I hadn't heard anything about a talk show.

But the next instant, the door to the office flew open, and Jenna stood there.

I soaked the woman in. When I had listened to her talking to the receptionist, I had imagined someone who was a lot like Velma. But the woman standing there was beautiful.

She had dark hair that she wore straight down to her shoulders. She was skinny and tall. She wore too much makeup and jewelry for my taste, but I could see where some people might like it.

"What's your name?" she demanded.

"I'm Elliot."

"You really work for Oscar Driscoll?" She didn't bother to hide the scrutiny from her gaze.

"I do."

"Why do you want to find Trina?"

"Her sister is worried about her." Oops. I was supposed to keep that quiet.

Her eyes narrowed. "Funny, she never mentioned a sister before."

I shrugged. "Did she ever mention much about her background?"

Jenna didn't say anything for a moment. "No, I guess she didn't. Come into my office. We can talk there."

I followed her inside the swanky room and sat down. The whole place smelled like rose petals, and pictures of fancy soirees were plastered around the room like trophies. Each of the frames were evenly spaced apart and level, creating a pleasant feature wall.

Jenna got bonus points for her attention to detail, at least.

"What exactly do you do here anyway?" I asked, turning back to the woman.

"We plan events," Jenna deadpanned, looking at me like I'd just graduated from the School of Stupid. She sat at her glass-topped desk and stared.

"Okay . . ." I supposed that *had* been an obvious question. "And what did Trina do for you?"

She folded her hands together, as if trying to look demure when she was really a cougar about to attack. "She was one of our sales reps. She met with potential clients and gave them quotes on how much it would cost to plan a party for them. She also helped with other tasks as needed."

I wondered just how well this job paid. Enough that Trina could buy herself a new condo and fancy jewelry? Or had she found a secret boyfriend, like others had suggested?

"Was she good at her job?" I asked.

"When she wanted to be charming, she could be. And when she wanted to fix up and make herself presentable, she could. Trina could be anything and anybody she wanted to be. It was all her choice. Her destiny was in her hands."

She sounded like a force to be reckoned with. "How did she even get this job? It wasn't exactly like her résumé was a perfect fit for you. She waitressed and worked retail before this."

I hoped my blunt question didn't offend Jenna. But my words were true. Trina's résumé seemed to contain a string of destructive patterns and behavior. Someone like Jenna would have noticed that.

Her jaw shifted to the side and her eyes narrowed. Classic signs of annoyance. "About six weeks ago, she showed up at one of my events and stepped in to help out as a server when we were short-staffed. We talked after that, and I agreed to give her an interview. We had a one-week trial run. She did fine so I decided to give her a chance."

"Then what went wrong?" Because it seemed like something had definitely gone wrong.

Jenna offered a half eyeroll. "I should have known after I called her references that she wouldn't last here. She has a reputation for leaving places and people without any notice. And that's what she did—right before one of our big events where we could have really used her help."

"I'm sorry to hear that. When was that?"

"About a week ago."

"I don't suppose you've heard from her since then? Maybe she contacted you wanting a paycheck or something."

Jenna let out a loud snort. "Oh no. Trina knew better than that. She knows better than to ever show her face here again, for that matter."

"Did you gift her with jewelry, by chance?"

"Jewelry?" Jenna's gaze narrowed as she stared at me, clearly giving me imaginary diplomas from that insulting imaginary school again. "No, why would we do that?"

"Someone did. Unless you paid her enough that she could afford it herself."

Something dark crossed Jenna's gaze. "We pay well, but not that well."

I was done here. I had no doubt about that.

"I see. If you hear from her, can you let me know?" I slid my card across the desk to her. I was becoming good at doing that, and I felt so professional each time.

"Of course." Jenna eyed me for a moment, and I wondered exactly what she was thinking. "Do you ever do any work on the side?"

"What do you mean? I have never been in the event-planning business, if that's what you're talking about."

"I've got something coming up tonight, and I need some extra help, especially now that Trina's left me shorthanded. You might even find that you like this line of work."

"When you say extra help, what do you mean? I'm not exactly event-planning material."

Based on the look the receptionist had given me earlier, I should head back to the jungle.

"Just having a pretty face helps. What do you say? We pay fifty dollars an hour for temp staff. And, no, that's not how much we paid Trina for a forty-hour work week. We're not that generous."

Fifty dollars an hour? That was very tempting, especially in light of my current financial situation. "Can I think about it?"

"Don't take too long." Her lips twisted wryly.

I nodded. I wasn't sure if working for Jenna would offer me any new information or not. But now I needed to meet Michael.

I PULLED my car one street over from our stakeout and then walked the rest of the way to Michael's minivan. He saw me coming and unlocked the door. As I climbed in beside him, I released my breath and leaned back.

I'd gotten that interview over with and hadn't totally made a fool of myself. Score one for me.

"Busy morning?" He stared at me as if waiting to hear about my tardiness.

"You could say that."

He didn't bother to hide the curiosity in his eyes as he took a sip of some foul-smelling coffee. "You want to share?"

I wasn't sure if I wanted to share or not. But it would be nice to have someone to run things past, and Michael knew a lot more about this stuff than I did. Maybe he would have some insight about what I'd learned.

I filled him in on my conversation with Trina's boss.

"Just like that she wants to hire you on the spot? To work some kind of event?"

I cringed when I heard the skepticism in his voice. "That's what she said. She pays fifty dollars an hour. Seems too good to pass up."

"I've never even heard of this company, and I've been in Storm River a long time."

"I think they just do galas, fundraisers, and parties. It doesn't sound like there's much risk of things being too illegal." Then, again, in this town, everything seemed like it could have a dark side.

Again, that wasn't a can of caterpillars I should open right now.

"You might be surprised." He raised his eyebrows.

"Or I might find answers," I reminded him, suddenly

craving some good coffee—like what I'd gotten at that place Hunter had taken me to.

"You're really determined to get to the bottom of this, aren't you?"

I shrugged. "Shouldn't I be? I'm supposed to work at things with all of my heart."

"Just be careful not to get too personally invested in any of these cases, okay?" His look almost reminded me of a concerned father.

"Of course not. I'm not personally invested. Why would I be personally invested?" My words came out a little too fast to be believable.

He gave me another look—one that I couldn't read. "I'm just saying . . . with everything going on with your sister, maybe you're transferring some of your emotions from your personal situation to this one."

"What do you mean?"

"Just that maybe you secretly hope someone will help you out the way you're helping out Rebecca."

Before we could talk about it any longer, Burke walked to his car and began pulling from his driveway. Maybe the change was good.

Michael was a little too adept at reading me, and I wasn't sure if I liked that or not. I was going to have to think about his conclusion a little more. Was that why I was doing this?

"What do you think?" I asked. "Is he going to the movies today?"

"How many movies can this guy see?"

"Looks like he's using his time off work to his advantage."

"Here we go again." Michael started the van, and we began following Burke again. Just as the past two days, Burke pulled into the movie theater lot and walked inside.

Michael shook his head beside me. "I can't believe this. We are never going to find any answers in this investigation."

"Or maybe there are no answers to be found," I reminded him. I, for one, was rooting to find one person in this town who was honest.

That wasn't true. I could list some honest people I'd met, starting with Michael. After what had happened in Yerba, I just felt so skeptical now. I didn't like that change in me, but I'd be a fool to deny it was there.

"Burke's former boss seems to think this case is worth pursuing, and he's the one who is paying us."

I couldn't argue with that. "What now?"

Michael stared at the theater. "I guess we can go back to the office for a little while. There's no need to sit out here and wait."

"You know what? I know this theory might sound crazy. But I think we should stick around here for a little while."

Michael glanced at me as if I'd lost my mind. "And why's that?"

I shrugged. "Just *intuición*."

"Honestly, I would rather hang out here in the parking lot

than go back into the office and talk to Oscar. He's in a rank mood today."

It was the first I'd heard about that. "Do you know why?"

"Maybe it has something to do with one of his ex-wives."

Interesting statement. "How many does he have?"

"Three."

I raised my eyebrows. "I had no idea."

"In case you didn't notice, Oscar doesn't like to talk about his personal life."

"No, for that matter, I really don't know much about him at all," I mused aloud. "Is he currently married?"

I hadn't seen a ring on his finger.

"He says he's sworn off dating. That he came to his senses."

Was that last part Oscar's words or Michael's opinion?

"Is that right?" I finally said. "I guess if he tried and it hasn't worked out three times, I could see why he might not want to do it anymore."

"Yeah, I could see that too. I've only had one serious relationship and it definitely changed my perspective." Regret edged Michael's words.

He was talking about Chloe's mom. I didn't know much about her, only that there was a story there. But Michael sometimes seemed like a closed book, and I didn't want to pry that book open. The pages seemed like they were damp and stuck together and likely to be damaged if I tried too hard.

"So what are we waiting here for?" Michael glanced out the windshield at the multiplex.

I let out a slow breath, trying to interpret whatever it was my intuition was telling me. "I don't know. But there's something about the way that Burke was walking that raised some alarms for me."

"The way he was walking?" Michael's voice climbed with doubt.

Here I went again—sounding crazy with my observations. But I loved details, and I couldn't seem to stop myself from picking out inaccuracies and shoddy imperfections.

"I can't really explain it," I started. "But Burke seemed a bit uptight, not like he was going to go to the movies and relax. Plus, he's wearing boots and a flannel shirt. It seems like most people like to wear more comfortable clothing to the movie theater. I may be totally off base, but let's just give my theory a shot."

"Why not?" He leaned back, as if he was in this for the long haul.

We waited a few more minutes, silence falling in between us. Nothing was happening outside except for more people going into the theater as others left. A movie must have just gotten out.

I scanned the crowds who exited, and I suddenly sat up straight. "Look at that."

Michael leaned forward. "What am I looking at?"

"That man there. In the crowd. Does he look familiar?"

Michael squinted and followed the line of my finger as I pointed. "The one wearing all black?"

"Yes, he's the one. Look closer."

Michael leaned forward until his forehead almost touched the windshield. The air slowly escaped from his lungs. "That's . . . Burke, isn't it?"

"He went inside, changed clothes, and then left again." I couldn't believe those words left my mouth. But we'd caught this man being deceitful. Part of me felt victorious.

"Why would he do that?"

The way Michael said the words left no doubt that he knew exactly why he would do that. Burke obviously knew that we were watching, and he was trying to lose us.

"Good job, Elliot." Michael cranked his van engine again. "Let's just go see what this guy really is up to."

I nodded, feeling surprisingly satisfied. Maybe we would finally get some answers and close the book on this workers' comp claim.

CHAPTER NINETEEN

WE FOLLOWED Burke out of town, down a country road, and we slowed when we saw him pulling into a wooded lane.

"We can't follow him down the lane," Michael said. "It's going to be too obvious."

"So what do we do?" I asked, anxious to hear what our next step would be.

"From here we go on foot, and we see what this guy is up to."

"It's a nice day, so I'm game." Even if it hadn't been a nice day, I was going to have to be game. Burke was going through a lot of trouble to cover up his whereabouts, and I wanted to know why.

Michael found a spot on the side of the road, just out of sight from anyone who might pass. We climbed out of his minivan, and he grabbed a bag he always kept with him containing his camera, binoculars, and a few other items I'd yet to see. Starting down the lane, we remained on the fringe of the trees.

"We have no idea how far this is, do we?" I glanced ahead and saw nothing but road and woods.

"Pretend it's a jungle hike." Michael glanced at me and smiled. "I know you really miss those."

At his words, memories of hiking with my dad filled me. I'd always thought that, when he'd met my mother, he'd been doing jungle excursions for wealthy tourists. Was that a lie also?

"I do miss those hikes," I finally said. "There's nothing like being in nature to make you feel close to God."

"Can't argue that," Michael said as we wove between the trees. "I've always wanted to go to South America, ever since I saw *Jungle 2 Jungle*."

"You should go one day." I smiled as I pictured him in the jungle, but the curl quickly left my lips. I had been about to say he should visit Yerba. It was the most beautiful country ever. But right now, the borders were closed and visiting wasn't a possibility. Maybe it would never be again. It felt almost like being disowned from your family.

"Yeah, maybe one day. I do love to travel."

"Do you?" I glanced at him, as my sneakers hit the gravel road and the sunlight filtered in through the trees. "I saw you as more of a homebody."

Surprise lit his eyes. "Really?"

Okay, I supposed people with his muscles and tattoos didn't fit the stereotypical homebody image.

"Maybe it's because you're a dad." I wondered what Michael had been like before Chloe was born. I knew he had played professional baseball, and I had the impression he hadn't exactly been a good boy. His gaze hinted at depths and secrets he kept closely guarded.

"Dads can still have fun too, you know."

I pushed a branch out of the way. "I have no doubt about that. But I know that your priorities also have to change, right?"

"You'll get no argument from me there. There's not a single decision that I make that I don't think about Chloe first." Just then Michael grabbed my arm and nodded into the distance. "There's a house over there. We need to make sure we stay quiet."

I nodded and clamped my mouth shut. I followed Michael as we headed deeper into the woods around the area. Thankfully, we'd both worn dark-colored clothing today so we wouldn't stand out too much.

We stopped at the edge of the foliage and paused. In the distance, we saw a one-story brick ranch house with a peach-colored exterior. The home was nothing fancy. But I had to wonder what Burke's connection was with this place.

We waited. As we did, Michael began touching things around us—the tree, some saplings, a vine.

My thoughts flashed back in time to the jungle.

"You know, my dad had a saying about being in the forest," I whispered.

"What's that?"

"Never pull on the rattan."

Michael stared at me in confusion. "What does that even mean? What's rattan? Something you make furniture with?"

"Rattan are these cords that hang down from the forest canopy. Visitors always want to pull on them. They think they're going to be able to swing on them, kind of like Tarzan."

"I can see where that would be tempting."

"What they don't know is what that string might be connected to. Sometimes, it could be coconuts. Sometimes, they're not connected at all and if you put your weight on them, they'll fall. Other times, pulling on them can bring down a nest."

"A nest?"

"Maybe a nest of spiders."

Michael nodded. "Interesting. But I'm not sure how that relates to this."

I shook my head. That was a valid observation. "Maybe it doesn't. Maybe I'm thinking about how you never know what you're going to get when you start tugging on things."

"An analogy. I like it."

"They're almost as great as acronyms, right?"

He said nothing.

"Anyway, maybe I'm thinking about this investigation into

Trina Morrison. Maybe I'm thinking about my dad—" I stopped myself.

"Your dad?" Michael stared at me as if he hadn't heard correctly.

I shook my head. "It's a long story. I guess I'm just wondering if I'm pulling on rattan but have no idea what I'm about to pull down."

"Seems like something good to ponder."

We quieted as people emerged from the garage.

Other cars were parked near the house as well. Five other cars, for that matter. Several people walked outside. Mostly men. And they were carrying . . . boards?

My suspicions rose. Maybe this Burke guy was lying. But we still needed more proof.

Michael pulled out his camera and began to focus the lens. As he did, I grabbed the binoculars and tried to get a better look myself.

Sure enough, that was Burke. And he carried a huge load of lumber on his shoulder.

He had been lying. His boss was right. He *had* faked his injury. What a loser.

But exactly what was he doing right now? Why go through all that trouble?

I continued to watch as the men began to set up a rectangle with the wood. They were laying out some kind of project.

"I think we have our money shots," Michael said, raising

his camera. "This guy is obviously a fraud. Now we just need to get these back to Oscar, and we'll let him handle the rest of it."

It took several days of doing nothing, but we finally had some answers. I almost wanted to do a cartwheel I was so excited. "We can put this case to rest."

Michael raised his hand in a high five. "We make a good team, you and I."

"You know what? I think so too." I really did. I was so glad he worked for Oscar.

"Now let's get out of here."

But just as we stepped away, I heard a sound that I was not supposed to hear.

My cell phone.

I'd forgotten to put it on vibrate. And now the happy tunes of *Dora the Explorer* began playing from it.

Michael had thought it was funny to program the tune a couple days ago when we got bored in the car.

I gasped and snatched the device from my pocket. I hit silent, but it was too late. The men in the distance glanced at us.

We'd been caught.

MY EYES MET MICHAEL'S. "I'm so sorry."

He ran a hand over his face before glancing at the men in the distance. "We need to get out of here. Now."

Without wasting any more time, we began darting through the woods.

But we were too late.

The men had heard us and were on our trail. I could hear them yelling. Could hear the branches snapping, the leaves swishing, the footsteps pounding.

I wanted to think we could outrun them, but the trees and thick underbrush worked against us.

"Freeze!" someone yelled. "I've got a gun. Don't make me shoot."

Michael closed his eyes, obviously unhappy as his steps slowed.

We both knew the truth. There was no need for us to run anymore. We might as well just try to talk this out.

Drawing in some deep breaths, we turned toward the men who'd stopped behind us. There were four of them, and one had an old hunting rifle aimed at us. The other three just stared at us, as if ready to get into a bar fight.

"Why are you trespassing on our property?" the man with the gun yelled.

"We're checking on Nolan's back situation." Michael raised his hands, looking more annoyed than he did scared. "You seem to be holding up pretty well after your injury."

Burke's eyes narrowed with realization. His thin body

seemed to stoop, as if guilt pressed on him, and he tugged at his shirt.

"My back?" Burke muttered. "My insurance company must have hired you."

Michael said nothing.

"This isn't what it looks like," Burke said.

"What it looks like to me is the fact that you are actually okay," Michael said. "But, meanwhile, you're taking home thousands from your employer based on a fraudulent claim."

I had to give Michael credit for not mincing words.

Burke turned to his friends. "I've got this, guys. Give me a minute."

The oversized men gave us one more death stare before stomping back toward the house. Then it was just Michael and me and Burke.

I was curious to know what he was about to say. How could he possibly explain this? Because I had a feeling that's what he was about to do.

"You want the truth?" Burke shifted, sweat covering his bony face.

"We would love the truth," Michael said. "Is that what you're going to tell us? You'll have to excuse us if we're a little skeptical."

Burke stepped closer. "It's exactly what I'm going to tell you. I know how it looks. And, yes, you did catch me carrying items that my injuries should have prevented me from being able to carry. I did hurt myself on the job."

"You can't tell it now." Michael stared at him, his gaze unyielding and unsympathetic.

"The truth is, I'm building a wheelchair ramp for my grandmother. Those guys helping are my cousins."

`I hadn't been expecting that one . . .

"It sounds like you're doing a good deed, but that still doesn't excuse your actions. If you're able to work, then you need to go back to work instead of drawing all of this money from your employer." Michael wasn't going to back down.

I had to admire his convictions.

"I'm using some of the money that I got to help Nana build this ramp," Burke explained. "I didn't plan on any of this, but since I got the money after my injury, I decided that I should put it to good use. I gave some to Nana, and my cousins came over to help me build the ramp. I shouldn't have carried that wood." Burke rubbed his back and grimaced. "Mostly, I'm just supervising. There's nothing wrong with that."

"If there's nothing wrong with it, then why are you pretending to go to the movies every day and secretly coming here?" I asked. Since I'd discovered that, I figured I could ask that question.

His eyes narrowed. "I'm not dumb, okay? I knew somebody was sitting outside my house every day. I also knew there was a good chance my insurance company might pull a stunt like this. I don't want everybody knowing my business. Now, could you not turn in those photos?"

Burke stared at us, something close to accusation in his eyes, almost like we were the ones who'd done something wrong.

Michael stared back, still unapologetic. "We were hired to do a job."

"How about, instead of worrying about your bottom line, if you think about the good of other people?" Challenge filled Burke's gaze.

"I make no promises," Michael said.

Burke looked in the distance, his lips pulling into a tight line and his eyes narrowing in obvious distress. "I don't know what I'm going to do if I lose this money from my claim."

"You'll figure something out, I'm sure. Something legal." Michael looked at me. "Come on. Let's go."

I gave one more glance at Burke before following Michael out of the woods and down the lane.

I waited until we were out of earshot before I said anything. "Do you think he's telling the truth?"

"I don't know if he's telling the truth or not," Michael said. "But, either way, he was carrying that wood."

"But maybe he was just carrying it to see how much he could pick up," I said. "Maybe he really is supervising."

Why did I want to see the best in people? That was going to hurt me on this job. I wanted so badly to believe that people were trying their best to be good people.

But I knew that wasn't always the case.

I couldn't read the look that Michael gave me. Did he feel sorry for me? Was that what his downturned lips meant?

"He could be telling the truth," Michael finally said. "But the fact that he's sneaking around to do this speaks volumes."

I couldn't argue with that.

I walked several more steps, trying to keep up with Michael and his fast pace. "So we're going to turn in those photos?"

"That's right," Michael said. "If Burke is telling the truth, then he can take this up with the people in charge of his insurance claim. It's not our job to determine if he's telling the truth or not."

Maybe what Michael was saying was true, but that didn't stop the unrest from sloshing in my chest.

How was Nana going to get her new ramp now?

CHAPTER TWENTY

MICHAEL and I went back to the office to give Oscar the update. When we walked in, Velma was arguing with Oscar about whether or not it was safe to eat roadkill. I pretended I didn't hear. I just couldn't handle that conversation right now.

Oscar looked up at us and folded his arms, a shadow crossing his gaze. "You're back early."

Michael raised his camera. "That's because we have answers. Caught Burke red-handed. I'll upload these to my computer and then send them to you."

"Excellent work. Thank you." Oscar's gaze swerved toward me, and the satisfied look in his gaze disappeared. "Elliot. Just the girl I want to see. I need to talk to you in my office. Pronto."

Something about the way he said the words left a bad

feeling in my gut. Usually these types of conversations didn't go very well, especially between Oscar and me.

Despite that, I followed him into his office and shut the door behind me. I didn't even take a seat before Oscar turned toward me. "What's this I hear about you doing some investigative work on the side?"

He leaned against his desk and stared at me, his arms crossed with subtle accusation.

Some of the blood left my face. "What?"

I'd heard him perfectly clear, I just needed to buy myself some time to process this.

"I heard from a 'little birdie' that you were doing PI work on the side."

"A little birdie?" The statement left me confused. What did that even mean? Was he talking about a parrot that repeated things?

Oscar glowered at me. "Stop avoiding my question. Are you or are you not doing PI work on the side? For that matter, are you working a case that I explicitly told you that we are not working, *muchacha*?"

"You mean Rebecca's case?" I fought the urge to close my eyes, but a rhyme already began forming in my mind.

It looked like I blew it. I had no choice but to do it. Someone had needed a hand, and I'd been the one with the plan. Unfortunately for me, Oscar wasn't a fan.

His eyes narrowed. "That's the one."

"I'm doing it as a good citizen, not as a PI. She desperately needs answers and—"

"I told you we weren't working that case."

The hardness of his voice made my throat tighten. "I know we aren't working it as a PI firm, but I didn't see any harm in—"

He pointed his nubby finger at me. "Part of the contract that you signed when you began to work here said that you would not take on any competing cases."

That had been in the fine print. I'd read it all. I was that type of person. "But I don't really see where this is a competing case—"

"This makes me feel like I'm unable to trust you, Elliot." He leveled both his voice and his gaze.

The sinking feeling in my gut sank even deeper. I hated disappointing people, and that was exactly what I'd done. "Of course, you can trust me. Just last week I saved your life by throwing myself in front of you as that gunman approached. What else can I do to prove my trust is deep enough to drown a mule?"

It was a Yerbian expression, but even I didn't quite understand it.

"I'm not even going to ask if you just called me a mule. Besides, when you saved my life, that was different. I'm talking about professional trust right now. I don't need you out there representing this firm and making a fool of yourself."

A fool of myself? My mouth dropped open. How

insulting.

I resisted the urge to cross my arms. That would only make me look defensive—and maybe even guilty. "I don't understand. When did I ever make a fool of myself? And how did you even hear about this?"

My mind raced through the possibilities. Who would have told him I was working this case? Who else knew? Michael? Jenna, Rebecca, Keith Freddie, Shawna.

Okay . . . it was a longer list than I wanted to admit.

What about Hunter? He was the only one who came to mind. But why would he do that? Had he done so hoping to take me off of the case?

I didn't know. But I didn't like this.

Besides, Hunter couldn't stand Oscar and vice versa. Nothing made sense right now.

"I'm sorry, Elliot," Oscar said. "You're fired."

My bottom lip dropped open. "You're firing me? Again?"

This was the second time in less than seven days. I was the responsible type—not the kind who repeatedly lost her job.

Oscar reached across his desk and grabbed a handful of pistachios. "Yes, I am. But this time it's for good."

"But Mr. Driscoll—"

"You can't talk me out of it. And don't send your watchdog in here either. Michael's not going to be able to go to bat for you this time, even if that's what he's really good at doing."

"But—"

Oscar straightened and sliced his hand through the air, sending pistachio shells over the floor. "That's it. No more talking. I need you to go. Now."

I FELT like I was doing the walk of shame as I left Oscar's office. Velma and Michael looked up at me in obvious curiosity as they stood chatting near the reception desk. Were they chatting ... or eavesdropping?

How much of that conversation had they heard? Oscar had a booming voice, and no doubt they'd been able to hear at least part of his reprimand.

"Again, huh?" Velma offered me one of her overblown frowns.

I didn't say anything. I just walked past her toward my desk. I still only had three personal items here—a picture of my family, a stress-relief ball, and a motivational plaque. I guess that was a good thing because it wouldn't take me that long to grab everything.

But now I was going to have to figure out an alternate work plan. I had to make money to help with my sister's surgery. Her life depended on it.

Apparently, I'd blown it again.

"I'm sorry, Elliot." Michael leaned in the doorway, showing off his muscles.

No, he wasn't trying to do that. It just happened naturally. Anyway . . .

He didn't offer to defend me this time. Maybe he even felt I deserved this. And maybe I did. At least I hadn't gotten him fired along with me. That was good.

"It was really nice working with you," I told Michael, heaving my purse on my shoulder.

Something flickered in his gaze. "Same here."

I gripped my purse and stepped toward the door, reminding myself I had nothing to be ashamed of. Doing the right thing should never be a reason to hang your head in shame.

"It was really nice getting to know you both," I said. "Thank you for accepting me."

"You too, sweetie." Velma offered a sad frown. "I'm having a barbecue tonight, if you want to stop by . . ."

I remembered her roadkill conversation earlier. "I'm sorry. I can't make it. Maybe another time."

Before I stepped outside, Michael joined me. "I'll walk you to your car."

Neither of us said anything as we walked down the sidewalk a little more slowly than usual.

"I know what you're thinking," I finally said. "You're thinking, I told you so. You warned me not to do this."

"You just still have a lot to learn about this business and about Oscar. Loyalty is everything to him. If you knew what he's been through, you'd understand it a little bit more."

I nodded, knowing I couldn't argue with what he said. Our pasts shaped all of us, sometimes in good ways and sometimes not. "It was really great to work with you, Michael. Maybe I'll see you around town."

A surprising sadness pressed down on me as I said the words.

Another one of those unreadable emotions fluttered through his gaze. "I hope so. Maybe you can come to one of Chloe's games sometime."

I nodded. "I would like that."

But something struck me. He almost seemed glad to see me go.

Why was that? Did he not think I was cut out for this job? Was the comradery we'd felt fake? Had I misread it?

"If you ever need anything, you know how to get in touch with me."

"I do." I smiled, even though the action felt forced. "Thanks again, Michael."

I really was going to miss him. Entirely more than I thought I would.

But with one last glance his way, I climbed into my car and pulled away.

I'd gotten myself into this mess, and now I needed to figure out what I was going to do.

There was only one thing that I could think of.

I needed to call Jenna and see if she still needed help tonight.

CHAPTER TWENTY-ONE

AS I WALKED into Elite Events two hours later, I felt like I had been ushered into the middle of a tornado.

Jenna was thrilled I was there to help, but we didn't have much time to waste. She instructed me to put on a black dress that came to my knees and fell slightly off my shoulders. My hair was swept back, makeup applied, and jewelry donned.

And I had been given heels.

I was so bad at walking in heels. I felt like a chicken about to peck someone.

"I really have to wear this to work this event?" I asked Jenna as I glanced in the full-length mirror situated in another office adjacent to hers, one that was more like a dressing room.

"We have a certain attire that is expected." Jenna observed me, smoothing the material near my shoulder. "But you look perfect for this job."

"I'm still not a hundred percent sure what I'm doing at this event tonight. I'm serving food or something, right?" I tried to picture myself doing that while wearing these heels, and I inwardly cringed at the thought of it.

"We'll explain everything to you once you get there. But you're going to be great. Just what we're looking for."

A bad feeling swirled in my gut, but I didn't know why. How hard could this be? These ladies were event planners, and I was just going to help the event run smoothly.

"How many of us are going to be there tonight?" I asked.

"Two." Jenna straightened my necklace.

"Only two? That doesn't seem like that many people for an event." Maybe I should have gotten more details before I'd shown up here.

"It will make sense when you get there." Jenna clapped her hands and turned, making it clear she was wrapping up this conversation. "Stacy, are you ready to go?"

Another woman appeared from the room beside ours, dressed equally as nice as I was, except her dress was a deep blue with a plunging neckline. I'd never seen her before, but she was probably my age, with a curvy body and silky blonde hair.

Stacy flashed a superficial smile. "Let's get this show on the road. I'll drive."

I'd kind of wanted to drive on my own. The act would, at least, give me a little assurance that I could leave early if I really wanted to. But Stacy had insisted on driving a nice little Lexus.

"This is a company car?" I glanced at the leather interior and decked-out dashboard.

"No, it's mine."

This job really paid well then, didn't it?

"Have you worked for Elite Events for a long time?" I asked as we headed down the road.

"About a year." Her long, elegant fingers gripped the wheel, showing off her rings and bracelets.

Great. Then she should know Trina. I needed to find a good opening to ask her about the woman in question. This could be my chance—because I wasn't giving up yet.

"Just remember to smile a lot," Stacy said. "And you're going to be great tonight. Everyone's nervous the first time."

"Other people are nervous about serving food at a party?" That shouldn't make the average person nervous, should it? Only clumsy introverts like me.

And I had to smile a lot too?

Things were not making sense to me right now.

Regret continued to pang inside me. I still couldn't get over being fired . . . twice.

Would I have changed anything if I could go back? I didn't know. I still felt like somebody needed to care about Trina, despite her rough past.

I started to ask Stacy more questions, but I didn't have time. We pulled up in front of the Boardwalk Yacht Club and Resort. I'd heard of this place before, but I'd never been here myself. I only knew that there was a lot of money inside these walls.

I'd heard rumors that people had to pay fifty thousand dollars just to get a membership at this place. Of course, in Storm River, people didn't even bat an eyelash at that amount of money.

My dad had worked maintenance at a similar resort when we'd moved here. I tried to avoid that place, though. There were too many bad memories there. It was where my dad had been when he'd had his supposed heart attack.

Stacy parked, and, without wasting any time, opened her door and climbed out of the car. "Come on. We don't want to be late. It's not smiled upon."

Something still didn't feel right with me. If we were planning this event, then where were our supplies? Was there another team already here overseeing the food and decorations?

Something told me this was a bad idea. Why hadn't I driven my own car?

I could barely keep up with Stacy as we hurried toward the front door, heels clacking against the asphalt—Stacy's more graceful than mine. But she was yammering on and on about what a nice place this was, what nice people were inside, and how well this job paid.

The well-paying part obviously meant a lot to her. She'd mentioned it more than once already.

I sucked in a breath as we stepped inside. The place was just as lovely as I would have imagined. And, then again, what wasn't lovely here in Storm River?

The ceilings were high, with chandeliers. Tapestries lined the walls. Lush carpet lay under my feet. No expense had been spared.

I cleared my throat. "Do I get an apron or something?"

"An apron?" A knot formed between Stacy's eyes. "Why would you . . . never mind. Just follow my lead."

We hurried through the lobby, toward a meeting space in the distance.

The inside of the meeting hall was swanky. No expense had been spared. Tables had been set up like for a banquet, and a stage stretched up front, just waiting for important people to speak there.

Had Elite Events planned all of this? I still expected to see trucks with their name sprawled across the sides outside— something to indicate the company's presence here.

There was nothing. Just the two of us.

"This way." Stacy nodded, making it clear I should follow.

Again, before I had a chance to ask any questions, she hurried away and I was expected to follow. More unrest jostled inside me. I gripped my little purse tighter beneath my arm, remembering that my cell phone was inside. If worse came to worst, I could call someone.

But who? I reminded myself I had no friends in Storm River. Not really.

I really should work on that.

Stacy stopped at a table, and one of the men there stood. My eyes widened as I recognized him.

Mr. Harrington.

His eyes also lit with recognition, followed by confusion.

"Mr. Harrington, this is Elle," Stacy said, placing a hand on my arm. "Elle, this is Mr. Peter Harrington. He is going to be your date for this evening."

"My date?" What sense did that make? I was supposed to serve food or hand out programs or make sure there was no trash on the floor.

Mr. Harrington took my hand and kissed it. "It's great to see you again, Elle. I had no idea you were coming. Or that Jono used Elite also."

I glanced at Stacy, a sick feeling in my stomach. "Wait. I . . ."

"We have a lovely dinner lined up and I know you're both going to enjoy yourselves so much. I'm going to leave you now." Stacy looked at me, a stern look of warning in her eyes. "But if you need anything, find me."

"Funny you said that, because I need—"

Before I could finish, Stacy sashayed away.

I was still trying to comprehend what had just happened. As I stood there, anxiety squeezed around me like an anaconda wrapped around my midsection.

I was Mr. Harrington's date? What sense did that make?

Was Elite Events some kind of dating service? And, even if it was, shouldn't I have some say-so in the matter? Why would I want to date someone who was old enough to be my father? In fact, this man had a daughter who was my age.

I glanced at the exits, wondering if I should make a run for one of them right now.

"Don't look so scared," Mr. Harrington said, leaning toward me. "It's just dinner. I needed someone to join me. It's a business thing."

"Dinner?" So I just had to eat with him, and I'd get paid fifty dollars an hour?

I still wasn't sure what to think here. Part of me wanted to call Michael right now and ask him to pick me up. He would do it for me if he could. I knew he would.

But dinner sounded innocent enough.

Right?

Before I could contemplate it too long, Mr. Harrington took my arm and turned back to the table, where he intro- duced me to the other couples seated there. I forced a smile, trying to look pleasant. I was quite certain that I looked more like a rhea with human teeth and lipstick.

The mental image made me cringe.

I needed to figure out what I was going to do.

A FEW MINUTES LATER, I placed a napkin over my lap and let out a deep breath.

I'd learned that this event was in honor of Senator Richard Bucks. He'd planned it as a way of saying thank you to all his top donors. The man himself was making the rounds through the room and would be speaking later.

Salad and dinner rolls were served, and the conversation around me turned toward the stock market.

I'd rather gouge my eye out than listen to hours of conversation about this kind of thing.

I tuned them out, and my gaze scanned the meeting hall. Finally, I spotted Stacy. She sat at another table beside another man. Except, unlike me, she was smiling and laughing as if she belonged.

Probably because she had known what to expect when she came here.

Unlike me.

"If you'll excuse me a minute," I said. "I need to run to the restroom."

Mr. Harrington smiled at me. "Of course."

I started toward the exit, but I made a quick right turn and went to Stacy's table. Her smile fell when she spotted me standing there.

"I need some help in the bathroom," I whispered through clenched teeth. "You mind giving me a hand?"

Her gaze shifted, and I could tell that was the last thing

she wanted to do. Despite that, she stood anyway, plastering on a fake smile and an even faker pleasant-sounding voice. "Of course."

As soon as we were away from anyone who could overhear, I leaned closer. "What is going on here?"

"Mr. Harrington needed a date," she said, not making eye contact. "You fit his type."

"Is this an escort service?" Nausea roiled in my stomach, and I stopped on the edge of the room.

"Not an escort service," she said through clenched teeth. She glanced around before pulling me out into the lobby. "Part of our business involves providing dates for wealthy men who need somebody to accompany them to business dinners and events."

I did *not* like the way this sounded. Not at all.

"The date ends here," she said. "You'll drive back to the office with me. It's nothing more. There's nothing illegal involved."

"But if this isn't illegal, then why didn't you give me a heads up before we came?" My words came out fast and heated.

"You wanted answers about Trina, right?" Her gaze narrowed as her impatient tone deepened.

My back stiffened. "That's correct."

"Do you want to know who Trina went out with during her last event with us?"

My pulse quickened. "I do."

Stacy leveled her gaze with me. "Mr. Harrington. Maybe this is your chance to get some answers."

My breath caught. Maybe it was.

CHAPTER TWENTY-TWO

AS I SAT at the table, listening to more talk about finances and things I didn't care about, a storm raged inside me. I shouldn't be here. I didn't care what Stacy said.

Maybe this truly was just a situation where I was expected to act as a date. But the insinuations that raced through my mind . . . it was going to make it hard for me to sleep at night. My dad would *not* approve of this.

I took a bite of my prime rib but hardly tasted it. What I wouldn't give for some mango and papaya right now. They were my ultimate comfort foods. I wanted to stuff my face full of the sweet fruit until I got a sugar high.

There were worse things to binge on.

Finally, the senator got up on stage and began talking about his election.

Again, I wanted to gouge my eyes out. Politics had left a very sour taste in my mouth.

I counted the minutes until he was finished.

Finally, he ended his speech twenty minutes later. As he did, a quartet began to play in the corner. Mr. Harrington turned toward me. "Would you care to dance?"

I wanted to tell him no. But maybe this would be my chance to talk to him. Still, I couldn't chase away the guilt and shame that I felt. My namesake would not approve of this.

But one dance couldn't hurt, right? Or was this how people always justified situations like this?

"Sure," I said, but my voice sounded scratchy.

He took my hand and led me to the little dance floor located in the center of the room. As the man's left hand went around my waist and the other took my free hand, disgust roiled in me.

"So how long have you lived here in Storm River, Elle?" His face was entirely too close as he asked the question.

"Not long. Only three months."

"It seems like you're fitting right in."

No doubt he was remembering my date with Jono.

Little did Mr. Harrington know just how out of place I felt in this area. I might as well be a monkey swinging around in the middle of a cement jungle.

"The area really is lovely," I finally said, finding a smidgeon of truth in my response. No doubt, Storm River was an exquisite town. The buildings were immaculate, the sandy beach was gorgeous, and the water pristine.

"I'm glad you ended up here," Mr. Harrington continued. "I appreciate you being my date for this evening. I'm so tired of trying to find dates on my own. Most people only want my money, and it gets exhausting."

"I can imagine you'd be in a difficult position to find someone to date," I told him, my throat tightening until I felt like I couldn't breathe.

His eyes narrowed in the dim light. "You're new at this, aren't you? Is this making you uncomfortable?"

"I am new at it, and it is making me a little uncomfortable. I'm sorry."

"It's okay. It's actually kind of refreshing to see. But I want you to know, this is just dinner. No strings attached."

"Yes, it's absolutely just dinner." I needed to make that clear.

He chuckled. "You are refreshing, Elle."

We continued to sway on the dance floor, but I made every effort to keep enough room for Jesus between us. That's what my mom had always said when it came to the opposite sex. And I'm sure she would have words to say about this situation I was in right now.

Very. Harsh. Words.

"I have a question for you," I ventured. There was no time like the present to ask. Maybe if I got this over with, I could get out of here.

"What's that?"

Here went nothing . . . "Was one of your dates from Elite Events named Trina?"

The smile slipped from his face. "Yes, actually, it was. I know Trina. The two of you even look a little alike."

"I've actually been looking for her," I said, trying to keep my voice casual. "She didn't, by chance, give you any hints about going out of town or anything, did she?"

He studied my face. "Are the two of you friends?"

I could tell by looking at the man that he was intelligent. He hadn't made millions of dollars by being a dummy. And I knew if I tried to feed him lies, that he would see right through them.

"Truth is, I'm trying to help someone who cares about her to locate her. I was hoping she might have told you something."

"And that is why you agreed to do this tonight . . ." He let out another low chuckle. "It makes sense now."

I shrugged. "It's kind of a long story, but, essentially, yes."

"I would tell you to leave right now, but doing something like this seems like a tactic I might use myself. Anything to get ahead, right?"

"I'm actually not that kind of person." But I did like to use every resource at my disposal.

"Yet you are. That's why you're here right now."

I stepped back from him, no longer interested in swaying on the dance floor. "I'm not."

He raised his hands. "I didn't mean to offend you. But you're feisty. I like that. Keep dancing before you draw attention to us. I'm a no-drama kind of guy."

He glanced around, and I realized even Mr. Harrington liked to keep up appearances. We all did in our own way, I supposed.

"I'm not sure it's a good idea that we keep dancing." I looked around and saw that some people were starting to look at us.

"I promise. I'll be good. And I didn't mean to insult you. I think it's a good quality. Your giving this quest to find answers everything you've got, and that's something that I admire."

I just needed to cut to the chase. "I would just love to hear anything that Trina might have told you."

We began swaying with the music again.

He looked off in the distance and let out a soft breath. "Trina seemed a little troubled, to be honest. We went out together on two different occasions like this. Dinner only. But the second time we went out, she wasn't herself."

My interest spiked. "Did she say if something was wrong?"

"I asked her. But she wouldn't say anything except that there was someone who was giving her trouble."

That was the second mention of this. "Did she say who?"

"No, I asked, but Trina wouldn't say. I told her I would try to help take care of it, if she needed me to."

"But she didn't go for it?"

"No, she didn't. She said she could handle it. She was that kind of girl."

"Did you see her talking to anybody else? Any clues as to where she might have gone after your last date?" Answers felt so close right now.

"I did see her talking to Frank Stephens over there." Mr. Harrington nodded with his head toward another man. "He owns Stephens Investments."

I glanced across the room at a fifty-something man who was probably thirty pounds overweight and sported reddish-brown hair. He laughed with two other men as they drank beer.

Stephens Investments? That sounded like a career for someone who had a lot of money . . . money to buy condos or jewelry maybe. Was he Trina's mystery man?

"Do you know what Trina and Frank were talking about?" I asked.

"You'll have to find that out yourself. I have no idea. But I thought I heard them saying something about meeting later on."

"When was this?"

"About two weeks ago."

"That's been very helpful. Thank you." Maybe I had another lead. At least it was something. Some progress was better than no progress.

I nearly stopped in my tracks as I saw another familiar face across the dance floor.

Was that . . . Oscar?

———————

I EXCUSED myself from my dance with Mr. Harrington and approached Oscar across the dance floor. I tapped him on the shoulder, not bothering to hide my irritation.

"Can I have a word with you, Mr. Driscoll?" I asked.

Oscar's eyes widened when he saw me. He paused from his dance with a woman I'd never seen before. "Elliot? What are you doing here, *chiquita*?"

"A moment of your time, please?"

He excused himself, and we walked to the side of the room, away from the dance floor.

"You frequent things like this?" I asked.

This did not fit the mental image I had of Oscar.

"Maybe." He shrugged, his cheeks turning a vague shade of pink. "Didn't expect to see you here, Jungle Princess."

I ignored his Jungle Princess jab.

Things began to click in my mind. He was the type who frequented things like this, who ran in these circles.

And that would mean . . . "You knew Trina, didn't you?"

"Trina was troubled." His lips twitched as he said the words.

I narrowed my eyes as facts began to fall in place. "She had something on you, didn't she? That's why you didn't want to investigate her disappearance."

Oscar didn't say anything, but I could tell by the look on his face that I was right. I felt a surge of victory, even though nothing about the situation had officially changed. Still, there was a lot to be said about the satisfaction found when things made sense.

Finally, Oscar shifted and lowered his voice. "Look, I like to keep my private life private."

"How could you not tell me that you knew Trina when you knew I was investigating?" I didn't try to hide the accusation from my voice. I didn't think my respect level for Oscar could sink any lower, but it had.

"Because it was my business and not yours." His voice hardened.

"What do you know about her? Do you know what happened to her?" Could Oscar somehow be involved? My breath caught at the thought.

"No, of course not." His words came out fast, harsh . . . maybe even a little shaken. "I talked to her once when she was with Mr. Harrington. That's it. Are you happy now?"

I wasn't anywhere close to being done or happy.

"Do you know anything about why Trina's missing?" I had to ask the question, though I wasn't sure if I could believe whatever he told me.

"No. Of course not." His nostrils flared, and his eyes widened as he stared at me, an incredulous look in his eyes. "You really think I had something to do with her disappearance? I think you're getting a little too big for your britches."

"You think I'm gaining weight?" Why would he bring that up right now?

"Gaining weight? What? No."

"I'm not sure what to think about you anymore." That was the truth.

He leaned closer and said, "You don't belong in this scene, Elliot."

"No joke. I didn't expect to be here exactly, but that's another story. I'm kind of out of a job right now."

He scowled. "It's not too late to leave, you know."

"You trying to get rid of me?" My hands went to my hips. What else was he hiding? Otherwise, why would he try to lose me now?

He lowered his voice. "I'm trying to get you out of here before you get in something too deep."

He knew something, didn't he? I wasn't even certain that it involved Trina. Maybe he just knew something about the underbelly of this town.

In most places, the underbelly might look filthy. But here in Storm River, the underbelly was dressed clean and sparkly, like something everybody wanted.

Like a wolf in sheep's clothing.

"Did Trina tell you that she was having trouble with somebody?" I asked.

Oscar let out a chuckle and ran a hand over his face. "Michael trained you well, didn't he?"

"Did he?" I wasn't going to let him off the hook this easily.

The fact that Oscar wasn't butchering any foreign words right now proved to me that he was nervous. He took every opportunity possible to mock me. I might be naïve to the ways of this new culture, but I wasn't stupid.

"She didn't tell me much of anything. Like I said, she and Mr. Harrington seemed to hit it off. But the last time I saw them together, about two weeks ago, she wasn't acting right. We were all at an event for an art gallery. She looked upset when she left, and she never came back."

"Is there anything else you can tell me?"

"Sure. You want a bone? I'll throw you one." He nodded across the dance floor. "I saw your friend Stacy go after her that last night I saw her."

CHAPTER TWENTY-THREE

IT TOOK everything within me to wait until the end of this event to find Stacy. But I managed to do it and to be a polite "date."

As the event wrapped up, Mr. Harrington kissed my hand as he walked me toward the door at the edge of the meeting hall. "Thanks so much for coming with me, Elle. I know it wasn't what you expected, but you did make for good company—and a very nice-looking companion, at that."

I nodded. "Thank you for respecting my boundaries."

He smiled. "Maybe I'll see you around town. Maybe even at that golf tournament next month."

I had no doubt that would be true.

A moment later, I found Stacy. As soon as we climbed into her car, I turned toward her, unable to hold back any longer. "The last time Trina was seen alive was two weeks ago at one of these events. You followed her when she left. Why?"

She didn't bother to start the car. "You like to get right to the point, don't you?"

"That's a detail you could have told me earlier. You know that Trina's been missing since then."

Stacy rolled her eyes. "Jenna said Trina had a habit of taking off. That it was risky to bring Trina into the company, and she hoped things would be different."

"So you really think Trina just left?" I had a hard time believing that. It seemed like she only did that when she had another plan—a better boyfriend, a better job, a better hair color, for that matter.

I hadn't heard about any of those things this time around.

Stacy's shoulders drooped as we sat in the parked vehicle. "Not really. I've been wondering what happened to her, and I guess I just wanted to believe that she took off on her own. It seems simpler than believing any of the alternatives."

I crossed my arms. "Tell me what happened that night."

"We were at one of these events together," she said. "It was a fundraiser for an art gallery in town. Anyway, I saw that Trina was getting upset about something. When she started to leave, I went after her to make sure she was okay. We have to look out for each other in this profession, if you know what I mean."

"What happened then?"

"Trina had just gotten a text message, apparently. She

said someone had been giving her a hard time, and she needed to put an end to it once and for all."

My breath caught. This was the information I'd been looking for from the start. "And what happened next?"

"She said she was going to go meet this person and be done with it. She didn't share any other details."

"Did she say where she was going to go meet this person?"

"She said something about going down to the waterfront. That there was a quiet place they could go to talk. I followed behind her for a while as we were driving—not maliciously, but we happened to be heading in the same direction. I saw her turn off."

"Where did she turn?"

"She turned toward a place called McCaverty's."

"McCaverty's? What is that?" I'd never heard of it.

"It's an old warehouse that was turned into a restaurant, but it's been shut down for a while. It's on the river, but up farther north, away from town. I wish somebody would do something with that place because, at one time, it was really rocking."

McCaverty's . . . wait. Rebecca had said she heard something about an investment opportunity Trina had at a place called Mac. What if Mac was actually McCaverty's?

Excitement pulsed through me.

I knew where I needed to head.

"Have I told you enough?" Stacy let out a sigh as she

looked at me. "Because I really want to get home and have a bubble bath right now."

"I think I'm good," I said. "Thank you."

I couldn't wait to keep investigating.

I DIDN'T WATCH a lot of movies, but I did know better than to set myself up to be a victim. I wanted to go down to McCaverty's. However, it was eleven at night, and I knew that wasn't smart.

Instead, I decided to text Michael.

I knew it was a long shot that he'd be able to meet me out there, but I decided to try anyway. To my delight, he texted me right back.

I'll be there in thirty. Just need to ask my mom to watch Chloe.

My hands trembled on the steering wheel as I headed out that way. I knew I probably should wait until morning. But I also knew my mind wouldn't rest until I had some answers. And if Trina was in trouble, there was no time to waste.

I'd gotten back to Elite Events with Stacy and exchanged a few terse words with Jenna. She'd seemed unaffected and told me she would put my paycheck in the mail.

I told her I would put this outfit in the mail as soon as I

got that paycheck, and then I grabbed my things and got in my car to leave.

According to my phone, I was only fifteen minutes away from this McCaverty's place. But, as I headed out of town, the darkness seemed to grow deeper around me.

Maybe this wasn't a good idea.

But Michael was already on his way there. Besides, it couldn't hurt just to take a look around, right?

Unless the Beltway Killer was involved.

My throat tightened at the thought. Serial killers weren't to be messed with.

But I hadn't found any evidence to prove he was part of this. Nothing yet indicated that the notorious madman had grabbed Trina.

But I'd be a fool not to acknowledge it could be a possibility.

Finally, I pulled up to an old brick warehouse. It was dark outside—really dark, despite the moonlight. I could barely see the name of the old factory painted at the top of the dark brick. I imagined this place in its heyday, and I bet it was quite the destination.

It had a prime location on the river, and it was far enough from the city to still feel peaceful. I bet on summer days, boats cruised past and a gentle breeze made everything feel a little easier.

As I stared at the building from my car, I realized there was no way I could check this place out. It was way too secluded. I didn't need my father's spycraft advice to know there was safety in numbers.

Had Trina really come here after that last evening of working for Elite Events? She seemed like the type who could be brazen, yet this didn't seem like any place for a woman—or man—to be alone.

Even when Michael got here, I didn't know if it was a good idea to check this out right now. I really should have thought this through a little more before I'd texted him.

For now, I would just wait for him to arrive and then we could talk.

But just as the thought entered my head, I heard a scream in the distance. It was followed by the distinct words, "Help me!"

CHAPTER TWENTY-FOUR

PANIC SURGED THROUGH ME. It had come from that old building. Could it be Trina? That seemed like too big of a coincidence. But someone was obviously in trouble.

Quickly, I called Hunter. If someone was in danger, law enforcement needed to get here—and soon.

"Hunter," he answered.

"This is Elliot. I'm at the old McCaverty's restaurant and factory, and I heard someone scream."

"I'll be right there. Don't attempt to go find this person alone. Understand?"

"I understand."

I ended the call and stared straight ahead.

But . . . what if someone truly was in danger right now? Should I just wait for the police to arrive? What if she was on death's doorstep, and I had the power to save her?

Then I heard it again. "Help!"

Someone desperately needed help.

My heart pounded in my ears. I knew I shouldn't, but I stepped from my car. I stared at the building, with the dark water glimmering in the moonlight in the background. An abandoned factory in the middle of nowhere at night . . . could this get any worse?

I glanced around and saw nobody else. No other cars. This place appeared abandoned.

But it wasn't.

Somebody was out there.

Someone who needed help.

What if it was my sister who was in danger? I'd want someone to step in, to intercede for her life. I closed my eyes.

Dear Lord, what should I do?

As I glanced down at the ground, I saw an old crowbar. It was almost as if the tool had been left there for me.

I scooped down and picked it up, gripping it like a bat.

Then I crept toward the building. At any time now Michael and/or Hunter should arrive.

They couldn't get here soon enough.

I reached the building, and I still saw no one and heard nothing else.

I walked alongside the exterior, my back toward the brick wall. My senses were on full alert for any signs of danger.

The only thing I could hear was my breathing and the

occasional soft footstep, made by me. I needed to get myself under control.

I was no good to anyone right now in this state. Fear was trying to control me.

As I reached the corner, I spotted the river. Old docks stretched there, docks that had probably been well used at one time. A pergola waited at the other end of the property, one that had probably been connected with the restaurant.

To my left, I saw the double doors leading into the warehouse. One was shattered.

The other stood open, almost as if inviting me inside.

That scream had come from inside that building, hadn't it?

I knew the answer.

It was yes.

The muscles around my spine tightened even more.

I didn't want to go in there. It wouldn't be smart of me to do so.

As if to lead me on, I heard it again. The scream. The desperate cry for help.

It was a woman.

Just what was happening inside that building? And if ordinary, everyday people didn't stand up for those who needed help, then who would? That's what had happened in Yerba. The middle class had disappeared, the poor had become poorer, and the powerful had used it all to their advantage.

I glanced at the time on my phone. Michael should be here any minute now. I prayed he made good time. I prayed that Hunter might be close too.

My heart slammed into my ribcage.

Thump.

Thump.

Thump.

I turned to the door. Stared at it. Wondered what was going on beyond it.

As I contemplated going inside, I heard a footstep behind me. Before I could turn, something slammed into my head.

Everything went black.

CHAPTER TWENTY-FIVE

"ELLIOT? ELLIOT? ARE YOU OKAY?"

I opened my eyes, just a crack.

"Elliot?"

I blinked. Was that . . . Hunter?

The man stood over me, concern knotted in the tight lines of his face.

I blinked again as confusion filled me.

Where was I? What had happened?

I glanced around. Darkness surrounded me. The air was dank. Danger crackled through the night.

A terrible throb pulsated throughout my head.

At once, everything slammed into me. I'd been standing outside the warehouse when . . . someone had hit me and everything had gone black.

But as I glanced around, I realized I was no longer

outside the warehouse. Was I . . . inside? Did that explain the smell? The darkness?

"Elliot?" Hunter said again, leaning down beside me with a flashlight in his hands.

New footsteps sounded behind him, and Hunter stood, drawing his gun.

A light bobbed in the distance.

"Stop right there!" Hunter yelled. "Police!"

"It's me. Michael Straley. Elliot Ransom called me."

The footsteps slowed, and Hunter shone his light on the man's face.

Michael.

It was Michael.

That's right . . . I'd texted him.

He raised his hands as if to say he was unarmed. As his gaze wandered toward the ground, he muttered, "Elliot . . ."

"Come stay with her." Hunter lowered his gun. "I need to find whoever did this."

Michael rushed to my side, crouching beside me.

As he did, Hunter strode deeper into the building.

I prayed the detective wouldn't get hurt.

"What happened?" Michael's eyes were orbs of concern. "Did you come in without me?"

I shook my throbbing head and pushed myself up. Michael put his arms behind me, supporting me. The floor was hard beneath me, almost like bricks. Dirty bricks.

"No, I was standing outside waiting for you," I mumbled,

closing my eyes as the throbbing became worse. "I heard someone scream and called the police. The next thing I knew, someone hit me on the head and everything went black."

Michael glanced around. "This is nowhere you want to be alone at night."

"Tell me about it." I let out a little moan.

More sirens sounded outside. A few minutes later, an army of people stampeded inside. Uniformed patrol officers rushed past.

Michael and I exchanged a glance.

Had Hunter found something?

Before I could ask very many questions, paramedics surrounded me and began to ask a million questions. Michael backed away so they could do their job, yet he stayed close, probably in case I needed him.

But my mind wouldn't stop working.

What had Hunter found?

Was it the woman I'd heard screaming? Had something happened to her also?

I wouldn't rest until I knew.

THIRTY MINUTES LATER, I insisted to the paramedics that I was fine and that I didn't want to be taken to the hospital.

I really did feel fine, and I really didn't want to pay the

hospital bill when this was all over. Sure, my head hurt. But I would get over it.

Hopefully.

I climbed down from the gurney where I had been sitting and stepped toward Michael. He took my arm and said nothing as I paced forward, paced toward the commotion in the distance.

Lights had been set up, and I could clearly see an old restaurant in the industrial space. There were high ceilings, bricks on all four sides of us, and old, dusty tables and chairs.

But the commotion came from down the hallway.

With Michael by my side, I wandered deeper into the warehouse.

I had a feeling that something very bad had happened.

"You sure you want to do this?" Michael whispered.

"I'm sure." But as the space became more narrow, as the stench around me turned rotten, I questioned myself.

He stayed beside me, almost as if he was ready to catch me if I fell. I followed the sound of the voices in the distance.

As I rounded the corner into the unrenovated area of the building, I stopped in my tracks.

Two legs jutted out.

My breath caught.

I wanted to stop but I couldn't.

I gravitated toward the body, straining to get a view of it.

My eyes widened when I turned the corner and a familiar face came into view.

Trina.

Based on the pallor of her skin and the horrible odor, I'd guess she'd been dead for a long time.

A cry escaped from my lips.

The next thing I knew, I found myself in Michael's embrace. He wrapped his strong arms around me. I closed my eyes, burying my face in his shoulder as I tried to forget the gruesome images that lingered in my mind.

"It's going to be okay, Elliot," he murmured.

Nothing felt like it was going to be okay right now. Trina was dead. In all my searching and investigating, I had really hoped to find her alive.

I didn't say anything. I was so thankful I had a friend here with me right now to hold me up.

I heard a footstep behind me and pulled away from Michael.

Hunter stood there, a frown on his face. "I'm going to need to get a statement from you, Elliot."

I nodded. As I touched beneath my eyes, I felt the moisture there. I hadn't even realized I'd been crying.

"What about the other woman?" I asked, trying to pull myself together.

"The other woman?" Hunter asked.

"I heard someone scream. Did you find anyone else?"

"Only Trina. She's been dead for at least a week," Hunter said.

More moisture pressed at my eyes. "There was no one else? I know I heard someone."

"Not that we've found," Hunter continued. "My guys are searching the rest of the warehouse."

I prayed no other dead bodies would be found. But who had that scream come from? If there were no dead bodies, did that mean . . . that the killer had grabbed someone else?

My head throbbed harder at the thought.

"Do you want to tell me what you were doing here tonight?" Hunter looked me up and down. "Dressed like that."

I glanced down and realized I was still wearing the black dress I'd donned for the event this evening. As I glanced at Michael, I saw the curiosity in his gaze as well. How much of my story could I really tell them?

I didn't want to tell them *anything*.

"It's a long story," I started, running a hand down my dress.

"We have time." Hunter stared.

I drew in a deep breath and resigned myself to get this over with. "I heard from a source that she saw Trina come this way about two weeks ago. It was the latest update I'd heard as to where Trina had last been seen. I texted Michael to meet me here. When I arrived, I realized I couldn't go inside alone. Then I heard someone screaming and crying for help. That's why I called you."

"Keep going," Hunter said. "You're doing fine."

I touched my throat, which now felt tight and swollen. "Do you know how she died?"

Hunter's gaze met mine. "It appears to be blunt force trauma to the head."

"Do you mean, like what happened to me tonight?"

Hunter barely nodded, but I saw it. When I did, my knees went weak. Things could have turned out so much differently for me.

Michael caught me, his arms wrapping around me before I hit the ground.

"Are you sure you don't want to go to the hospital?" Hunter asked.

"I'm positive. I want to do whatever I can to catch this guy." My gaze met Hunter's. "What if the killer was here and grabbed somebody else?"

"We've been looking for evidence of a struggle," Hunter said. "We haven't found anything recent yet. We'll keep looking."

My gaze went back to Trina one last time. That's when I saw them.

The beer cans near her body.

"Keith Freddie drinks that same beer," I muttered. "I saw cans at his apartment."

Hunter's eyes widened as he nodded. "Noted."

"Does Elliot need to stay here?" Michael asked, his arm still around me.

"She can go." Hunter's hard gaze met Michael's. "I'll call her if I need anything else."

Michael started to lead me away, but I paused. "By the way, do you know who owns this building?"

"A man named Frank Stephens. Why?"

He was the man Mr. Harrington had seen Trina talking to on their last date. He'd heard them saying something about meeting later.

I closed my eyes. Was Frank behind all of this? Had he followed me from the gala, somehow knowing I was onto him?

It seemed like a good guess.

I told my theory to Hunter, and he promised to look into it.

With that, Michael began to lead me out of the building. First, Hunter gave me a long, lingering look that spoke volumes—volumes about just how close I'd come to dying tonight.

What had happened tonight would stay with me for a long time.

CHAPTER TWENTY-SIX

MICHAEL INSISTED on driving me home, and I couldn't argue. I knew I was in no state to be behind the wheel. I'd have to figure out how to pick up my car later.

But as we settled into his minivan, Michael made no effort to go anywhere.

"You want to tell me what really happened tonight?" Michael finally asked.

"What do you mean?" As usual, I was trying to buy some time. When would I learn that didn't work? It only delayed the inevitable.

He glanced down at my outfit. "Why are you dressed like that? And how did you find out that this was the last place that Trina was seen?"

"It's a long story." Dread pooled in my gut. Could I rewind this day?

"I've got time."

Michael was like a subtle interrogator. He would get this information out of me, and I could make it as easy or as painful as I chose.

I just needed to get this over with.

"I took a new job, but I had no idea it was with an," I wiped a hand over my lips, muffling my words as I said, "escort service. Turns out Trina had worked for them too. I talked to one of the girls she worked with, and she said she saw Trina heading this way on the last night she was seen."

My words—the ones that weren't muffled—were rushed. On purpose.

Michael stared at me. "Say that again?"

"I didn't mean to," I blurted. "I thought I was working for a party planner and that I'd be serving food."

"You're telling me that Elite Events is actually an escort service?" His eyebrows shot up.

"I don't know. I guess so. I mean, they plan parties too. But they have a new arm of their business that provides dates to wealthy clients in the area. They say it is only dinner and nothing else."

"Yeah, right." Michael shook his head. "And I'm Babe Ruth."

"A candy bar?"

"Never mind."

I cleared my throat, knowing this conversation wasn't

done. "When I found out what was going on, I made it clear that I was just there for the food."

"How did that go over?"

"Mr. Harrington seemed very understanding."

"Wait. Mr. Harrington was your date? He uses an escort service?" Michael's voice rose.

"Trina had been his date several times, apparently."

Michael shook his head. "Nothing in this town should surprise me anymore."

"And Oscar was at this event. I didn't see him as the type."

"There's a lot about Oscar you probably don't know." He let out a breath as he stared at me. "You put yourself in a bad situation tonight, Elliot."

"I know, but, like I said, I didn't know. I thought I was just taking a job with an event planner. Then I found out that Trina was mixed up in it, and I thought maybe I could get some information."

"It's a good thing you're still alive." He looked at me, and something flashed in his gaze.

What was that? Genuine concern? But as he squeezed his lips together, it almost looked like he wanted to say more but didn't.

What was on his mind?

I shrugged and didn't ask. "I'm very thankful to be okay. Thank you for coming. I'm sorry to pull you away from Chloe. I knew I shouldn't come here alone. I just didn't know what to do."

"You did the right thing by texting me. Maybe the police and the medical examiner will be able to get some information off of Trina. I know closure will mean a lot to her sister."

I stared out the window at the ambulances and police cars still parked around the warehouse. "I can't believe she's dead. I was hoping that . . ."

Michael squeezed my arm. "I know. We all were. But now we just need to find out who her killer is."

"The Beltway Killer . . . he doesn't kill by bludgeoning somebody to death, does he?"

"No. His preferred method of murder is stabbing."

"So Rebecca was wrong. Trina wasn't grabbed by the Beltway Killer." As I said her name I straightened. "Someone is going to have to tell Rebecca what happened."

"Why don't you let the police do that?"

"I think she should hear it from me."

Michael shook his head. "It's past midnight. Do you even know where she lives?"

"No, but I have her phone number."

"You can't call her out of the blue and tell her you need to stop by after midnight. Trust me, Elliot. Let the police handle this."

He had some good points. But I could call her in the morning. See how she was doing. Offer my condolences then.

"Okay." I nodded. "That's what we can do."

And with that, Michael took off toward my house. But my

soul still felt unsettled.

AS I LAY in my room that night, I thanked God that He had sent someone like Michael into my life. I'd been praying for a good friend since I came here, but I never expected it to be someone like Michael. Yet he was honest, loyal, and there for me.

Now that I'd been fired from my job with Oscar, I didn't know what our friendship would look like. Was he just a friend of the moment? If we really had to work to see each other, would we?

I didn't know the answers to those questions. I hoped so, but Michael almost looked happy when Oscar fired me. Despite that realization, he *had* been a real lifesaver tonight. The two thoughts didn't mesh.

My mind kept replaying everything I'd learned in the past day. Did I have enough information to find Trina's killer? I hadn't been hired to do that but . . . it just seemed like I should.

I sat up in bed and pulled my notebook in front of me so I could jot down my thoughts.

I thought about what I did know.

Trina wasn't a faithful friend. She would rather chase bigger and better opportunities.

Someone had been bothering her, though I didn't know

who that person was.

The night she disappeared, she'd met somebody at McCaverty's. The fact that she had met someone there indicated that it could be someone she trusted.

She'd been wearing new jewelry and living in an expensive condo complex.

She'd been bludgeoned approximately two weeks ago.

I tried to mentally tick off who my suspects might be.

The first person who came to mind was Mr. Harrington. He was a person of means and wealth, and no doubt he valued his reputation. Had Trina done something to put that in jeopardy?

What about Keith? Trina had left him, and Keith seemed to have an edge to him. His truck had run me off the road. Cans of his brand of beer were found at the crime scene. He'd even burned all of Trina's clothes. Could he be responsible for this? Had he killed Trina in a fit of jealousy?

Or what about the other man Mr. Harrington had mentioned? Frank Stephens? I hadn't even begun to investigate him yet. But maybe I should.

Either way, this wasn't the way I had wanted things to end. I was so thankful that I was okay and that the killer hadn't finished me off also. Had I just happened to arrive as the killer was planning another move? Who had that scream come from?

I had so many questions. Maybe tomorrow would offer more answers.

In the meantime, I opened the jewelry chest that my father had made me and pulled out the journal he'd left hidden in the secret drawer. I wanted to see what kind of wisdom he had jotted down there for me now.

In the morning, I was going to jump right back into this investigation. I didn't care what anyone had to say about it.

CHAPTER TWENTY-SEVEN

FIRST THING IN THE MORNING, I tried to call Rebecca. She didn't answer.

I figured she was either in class or that the police had delivered the news about Trina and she was in mourning.

I should have gotten her address from her, but I hadn't. I made a mental note to get more information from nonclient clients before taking any more cases.

Not that I would probably ever do this again.

I would try to call her later.

In the meantime, I wanted to swing by Elite Events to drop off my clothes and jewelry from last night, as well as to talk to Jenna again. I'd checked their website and saw they didn't open until ten today.

Instead, I took the bus to the warehouse where I'd picked up my car. Then I headed to Frank Stephens' office. The building was located in downtown Storm River. It was a three-story structure painted a clean white, and it had neat flowerbeds out front.

I wanted to talk to him and see if he had anything to do with Trina's death.

I'd used a tactic Michael had taught me—I'd checked the man's social media pages. Through that, I'd discovered that Frank was in a meeting at his office this morning and had a lunch date later with a colleague at a restaurant across town.

I'd also discovered what kind of car he drove—it had been in a picture he'd posted. As I pulled in, I saw the BMW in the parking lot. I took that as a sign Frank was probably here.

Glancing at my watch, I also noted that I probably had between thirty minutes to an hour until he left for his lunch meeting.

I walked over to the newspaper stand, stuck some change into it, and pulled out *Storm River Daily*. What could blend in more here in this town than a girl sitting on a bench reading the newspaper?

It seemed like a good theory, at least.

The weather was cooperating. It was downright perfect today, with blue skies, bright sunshine, and a moderate temperature of sixty degrees.

I opened the newspaper and held it in front of my face, occasionally glancing around to keep an eye on things. People were still coming and going from the building, but I hadn't seen Frank Stephens. I had looked up his picture online last night so I could more easily identify him.

Finally, fifteen minutes later, someone emerged from the building.

I sucked in a breath, and a surge of victory rushed through me.

Frank Stephens stepped out the front door and walked toward the parking lot, a limp to his step. Someone had pulled his BMW up to the entrance of the building.

This was my opportunity. I put the newspaper down and rushed toward him. "Mr. Stephens!"

He paused and glanced at me for a moment before frowning. "Can I help you?"

"I desperately need to talk to you."

"I'm sorry. But I don't have time to—"

"It's about Trina Morrison," I blurted.

He froze, his hand on the passenger door as he glanced around to see if anybody was listening. A thin layer of sweat beaded on his ruddy skin.

"I don't have anything to say about her." He reached for the car door, but I nudged myself in front of him.

"Did you know she was found dead last night?" I rushed.

"That's not something I would like to discuss with you." His nostrils flared—just barely.

But I'd seen it. I knew he was irritated and that I'd struck a nerve.

"I know that you are one of the last people to be seen with her," I continued. "Would you care to explain that?"

His cheeks turned even redder as he turned toward me. "This is a police matter. I don't know who you are, but—"

"I am someone who was hired to find her. And now I want to find her killer."

He pushed me out of the way, opened his car door, and pointed to the interior. "Get in."

I stared at his BMW, wondering if that was a good idea or not. Would I end up in a warehouse dead just like Trina had?

He seemed to read my thoughts, and he sighed. "I'm not going to hurt you."

I swallowed hard and glanced around. A security guard was watching us from the entrance of the office building. A chauffeur sat in the front seat as well.

If I did disappear, at least those two would have seen me with him.

However, they were on Frank's payroll.

The decision pulled at me until I finally got in the car with him. Certainly, this man was smart enough not to kill me after there were witnesses seeing me get into his vehicle.

At least, that's what I was hedging my bets on.

He climbed in beside me and slammed the door. Then he rattled off a location to his driver, and we took off.

"What do you want to know?" He turned toward me, all business. "And who are you?"

"My name is Elliot."

"Who do you work for?" he continued as we headed down the road.

I swallowed hard, hating to not tell the complete truth. But, in this situation, I didn't know what else to do. "Oscar Driscoll."

His eyebrows shot up. "Good old Oscar, huh?"

"I know there was something there between you and Trina."

He chuckled and shook his head. "*Something* might be a bit of an exaggeration. We went out a few times."

"Were you the one buying her the jewelry?"

"I was. She liked shiny things. It kept her happy."

"Did you pay for her condo?" The questions kept pouring from me like water from a spring.

He tugged his collar. "Maybe."

"But you only went out a few times?" That did not add up in my mind.

"I liked her. She was pretty. She was fun. But I wasn't looking for anything serious."

"Then why buy her those things?"

He let out another long breath. "To keep her happy. To some people, it might seem like a big deal. But to me, I make more in a day than it cost me to pay for them. It wasn't a big deal."

I couldn't be too quick to buy his story. Were people's motivations ever that simple? "To me it almost seems like you might have been appeasing her or trying to keep her quiet."

He glanced at me, and I knew I'd hit on something.

"My ex-wife is trying to get more money from me, okay? If she knew that I had been out with Trina while we were still married . . . she would have ammunition and get more than her fair share of cash. I bought Trina things in order to keep her silent. Happy now?"

Not really. I found this man despicable. However, that wasn't a surprise.

"What about McCaverty's? What was her connection to that place?"

He let out a deep breath. "That's how Trina and I met. She learned that I owned the building and approached me about wanting to fix it up. To make it great again. To bring it back to its days of glory. She was trying to get me to let her renovate the place and turn it into a club."

"What did you tell her?"

He shrugged again, obviously not wanting to be committal. "I was considering it."

"But she was still holding that leverage over you, wasn't she?"

"Look, she had good ideas. If she just found the right ways to channel her energy, she would be a force to be reckoned with. I thought this might be a way to keep her occupied."

"And to keep her out of your hair." I shifted. "But it also sounds like she was getting more expensive for you."

His gaze cut into me. "I didn't kill her."

"But she was found on your property."

"I *couldn't* have killed her. I had knee replacement surgery three weeks ago. This is my first time coming to work since then. I was barely able to walk. Ask anybody. They'll tell you it's true."

I *had* seen him limping. But I would verify what he told me.

"I have already been through all this with the police this morning," he said. "And I have nothing else to say to you."

The driver pulled up to a building, and Frank opened the door. "I have a meeting to get to. My driver will take you back to your car, though. Have a good day."

———

I WAS STILL MULLING over what Frank Stephens had told me when I went to Elite Events to give Jenna a piece of my mind.

Just as I expected, she didn't care.

"I asked you to do a job for me," Jenna explained as she sorted through some papers in her office. "And that's what you did."

I stood in front of her, my entire body tense and my mind on edge. "What you're doing borders on being illegal."

"I never asked any of my girls to do anything illegal.

What happens after hours is up to them." Jenna cast me a cold stare as she continued to look through the papers.

"Is there anything else about Trina that you're not telling me?"

"I didn't know Trina well, and hiring her was a mistake. Mr. Harrington seemed to like her, though. We like to keep our clients happy."

"And Frank Stephens?"

Jenna stared at me. "He's not one of her clients."

So Trina must have met him on her own somehow. The money that he had given her must have offered enough of a cushion that she felt comfortable leaving Keith and purchasing that condo. It had given her the push she needed to get a new job as well, at least until her new business venture with McCaverty's worked out.

I figured I'd gotten everything I could from Jenna and stood. "Thank you."

She glanced up at me. "No, thank you for keeping this between you and me."

I tilted my head, unsure what she was talking about. "Keeping what between you and me?"

"This new little branch of my business. I appreciate your discretion."

"Who said I was going to use discretion?" I narrowed my eyes, wondering why she'd put words in my mouth.

"Now that you are officially an escort yourself, I can't see you wanting to implicate yourself in all of this." Satisfaction shot through her eyes like laser beams.

My mouth dropped open. Jenna was a manipulator. I *hated* manipulators.

I didn't say anything for a minute. I didn't know what exactly I should say, and I was certain that, if words left my lips, I'd end up regretting them.

Instead, I shook my head. Honestly, I felt sorry for the woman. If she couldn't have a business she was proud of, why have a business at all?

Then the irony of my thoughts hit me. My mom had no idea I was working for a PI. Or that I had been working for a PI, I should say.

I'd known she would worry too much so I hadn't told her. Instead, she'd assumed it was a law firm, and I hadn't bothered to correct her.

I guess I shouldn't be so quick to judge Jenna now, should I?

Still, I wasn't going to give Jenna the satisfaction of a response.

I did have one more thing to ask her, though. "You did hear that Trina was dead, didn't you?"

Jenna stared at me, her gaze going still. "What?"

"Have you not seen the news today?"

"I don't watch the news. It depresses me."

"Well, I'm sure the police are going to come here to question you."

Her face turned a little paler. "How . . . ? When . . . ?"

"Her body was found last night. Blunt force trauma to the head. The last place she was at before she died was at one of your events. Do you care to explain that?"

Jenna shook her head, some of her cockiness wearing off. "I have nothing to do with her death. I can assure you of that."

"You don't need to assure me of anything," I told her. "It's the police that you're going to have to tell that to." I turned to leave when I heard her call my name.

"By the way, you and Stacy left together last night, right?"

I couldn't be sure, but that looked like trepidation in Jenna's gaze.

"That's right. Why?"

"Because she hasn't been answering her phone this morning," Jenna said.

A chill washed through me. Maybe that didn't mean anything. But my gut told me that it did.

"Is that unlike her?" I asked, ignoring the ache in my throat.

"It is. I was hoping she told you she was going somewhere."

"She didn't mention anything except wanting a bubble bath."

Jenna's face turned even paler.

"You need to call the police," I told her. "Now."

CHAPTER TWENTY-EIGHT

I DIDN'T WANT to be at Elite Events when Hunter arrived —provided he was the one who showed up. I knew he usually worked in the evenings, but I figured this was his case so he'd be the one to come.

He was going to have questions for me.

But if I stuck around to answer them all, I couldn't do my own investigation. I figured one way or another Hunter would track me down. For now, I had other things I needed to do.

My brain was racing from everything that I learned. Had the killer grabbed Stacy? What sense would that make? It made me question everything I'd assumed about the killer's motives.

So many emotions clashed inside me. At a time like this, I shouldn't care about my reputation. But sooner or later it was going to come out that I had worked for Elite. I didn't know what people would think about that or what they would assume about me. But I didn't like it.

And Jenna had known that would be the case.

I set aside my anger and tried to think clearly for a minute as I headed down the road.

Quite possibly, I could rule out Frank Stephens. I still needed to verify that he had knee surgery, but that should be easy to do.

Who else might be responsible? It seemed like I was getting closer to answers. Otherwise, why would someone slash my tires and steal Keith's truck to run me off the road?

I had a hard time believing the person responsible was someone I hadn't come in contact with yet.

And then there was Stacy . . . what could've happened to her?

My phone rang then, and I hit the speaker button when I saw Michael's number. I really hoped he didn't give me another lecture. I couldn't handle it right now.

"Where are you?" he asked.

"I'm driving."

"Can you pick me up?"

"Aren't you working today?"

"Oscar doesn't have anything for me, so I'm taking the rest of the day off."

"And you want to ride around with me? Need I remind

you that Oscar fired me because I was doing this work off hours?"

"I can handle Oscar. Right now, I want to help you before you get yourself in more trouble. Can you pick me up?"

"Where?"

"At Oscar's office."

"I'll be there in fifteen."

I couldn't deny that I felt better knowing Michael was going to be with me. I could really use his perspective right now on everything that was going on.

As soon as I ended that call, my phone rang again.

This time it was Hunter, just as I expected.

"Elliot—" he started.

I got right to the point. "I know what you're calling about. Stacy dropped me off at Elite Events last night and said she wanted to go home to take a bubble bath. Otherwise, I have no idea where she is."

Hunter remained quiet for a moment. "That was direct."

"I know you don't want to waste any time with this. But I promise you, if I think of anything that I think is relevant to her disappearance, I'll let you know."

"Why are you in a rush?"

"I'm following another lead."

"Elliot . . ."

"I'll be careful. I promise."

"If you find anything else out, let me know."

"I will." I ended the call and tossed my phone into the seat beside me.

Now I needed to talk to Michael.

"SO YOU CONFRONTED FRANK STEPHENS?" Michael stared at me as we sat in my car outside Oscar's office building. "You do know who he is, don't you?"

"If I let a person's status stop me from questioning them, then I would never talk to anybody in this area."

"True that." Michael leaned back.

I had already told him everything that I knew.

"What should I do now?" I asked.

He let out a long breath. "It sounds like you have gotten yourself into a pickle."

"What do pickles have to do with this?"

"Never mind."

Another Americanism, I had to assume. "Anyway, I found one dead body last night and then I find out somebody else is missing? How can I let it drop now?"

"What about Rebecca? Did you ever hear back from her? How is she handling all of this?"

"I tried to call, but she didn't answer. I can only imagine she's grieving or that she's trying to pretend like everything is okay by continuing on with life. Maybe she had class this morning."

"Did you think about going past her home?"

"I did, but I actually don't have her address." I tried to hide my embarrassment over the snafu. I was such an amateur, and stuff like this proved it.

"I can probably figure that out for you." He pulled out his phone.

"Really?"

"Elliot, I am a licensed PI. I should hope I can do things like this."

"I'm not going to stop you then."

He typed several things into his phone before letting out a grunt.

"What is it?"

"I actually can't find Rebecca's address. But I do have an address for Trina's mom. Maybe we should start there."

"I think that sounds good."

Michael put the address into his GPS, and, ten minutes later, we pulled up in front of a house on the edge of Storm River. It actually wasn't terribly far from my own home. In other words, it was on the wrong side of the tracks.

I pushed down my nerves as we walked up the broken sidewalk to the crooked front door. If the situation was different, I might ask the homeowners if I could tighten the hinges for them. Didn't things like this drive everyone crazy?

Then I remembered that nobody inside would care right now about the door being even. They had much greater problems at hand. Compassion pounded inside me.

I understood grief. I knew what Trina's family had to be going through. And I didn't take that lightly.

I didn't see a doorbell, so I knocked. Then I waited. Several minutes later, I finally heard footsteps inside.

The door opened, and a woman with red eyes stared at us.

"Not today," she started, waving a tissue-clad hand in the air as she reached for the door to shut it.

"Wait!" I called. I didn't know who she thought we were, but I desperately needed to talk to her.

"What do you want? I'm not in the mood to buy anything." She crossed her arms, and I could tell her patience was already wearing thin.

"We're not selling anything. I'm looking for Rebecca."

The woman stared at me with her red-rimmed eyes. "Who's Rebecca?"

I glanced at Michael. Maybe we did have the wrong house. But if that was the case, why was this woman crying? And why did she look so much like Trina?

"Are you Trina Morrison's mom?" I asked.

"I am. But I don't know a Rebecca."

I stared at her, unsure what to say as I processed her statement. Was that her grief talking or was she telling the truth? Nothing made sense right now.

"What's going on here?" the woman asked.

"Trina's sister, Rebecca, hired me to find her," I said.

The woman stared at me, looking a bit dumbfounded as

her bottom lip parted from the top. "Trina doesn't have a sister named Rebecca. Now, if you don't mind, I have a funeral to plan."

"But—"

Before I could finish the question, the woman slammed the door.

But I just felt like she had slapped me. What did she mean when she said Trina didn't have a sister? It didn't make any sense.

I felt like my whole case had just been turned upside down.

CHAPTER TWENTY-NINE

"MAYBE REBECCA IS DEAD TO HER," Michael suggested as we sat in my car on the street in front of Trina's mom's home.

"I don't know," I said. "She looked pretty perplexed when we brought up Rebecca's name."

"But what sense would that make? Why would Rebecca pretend to be Trina's sister?"

"I have no idea." I ran a hand through my hair, trying to ignore the way my head pounded right now. "But you said you couldn't find a record of an address for her. It's almost like Rebecca doesn't exist."

None of this made any sense. No matter which way I tried to look at it, I couldn't come up with any logical explanation for this turn of events.

"I guess you didn't think to research your client, did you?" Michael asked.

I felt my cheeks heat. "I didn't know I was supposed to."

"It's never a bad idea."

I turned to him. "Even if Rebecca isn't Trina's sister, I still don't see how this all fits. Why would she pretend to be Trina's sister and ask me to find her?"

"I have no idea. Maybe if we figure that out, we'll figure a few other things out also."

I let my head fall back against my seat as I tried again to think this through. No amount of time or binging on fresh fruit would help me through this, I was afraid.

"Maybe we can do a little more research on Rebecca," Michael suggested. "What do you know about her?"

"She said she was in college. That she worked at a fast food restaurant—McDonald's." I searched for more things to say but came up blank. "Okay, so that's it. I guess she didn't actually say that much."

"She didn't say anything else about herself?" Michael clarified.

"Just about how worried she was about Trina. And she also said . . ." I stopped myself. What I was about to share couldn't be significant, right?

"What?"

"She said none of Trina's friends liked her, so I shouldn't tell them she was the one who hired me."

"So nobody else you've talked to has mentioned Rebecca?"

I shook my head. "No. I didn't bring her up—except to Detective Hunter. He said she'd come into the station."

Michael let out a long breath. "I have to admit, I'm intrigued. I have no idea what's going on here, but it's not good."

"Maybe Rebecca knew who the killer was, but she couldn't come forward and say that for some reason. So she hired me, hoping I could pave the way." I knew my words sound farfetched.

"But what about the police?" Michael said. "Didn't she go to the police and ask them for help? We just need to think these things through."

"I agree." But as all the questions collided in my head, I felt at a loss as I tried to figure out what to do next.

FIFTEEN MINUTES LATER, Michael and I were inside The Board Room. We needed a place with good Wi-Fi, and this fit the bill.

Michael was looking into Rebecca, and I was trying to confirm Frank Stephens' alibi.

In the meantime, Michael had ordered what he called his "thinking board." It was a charcuterie board with hot dogs, pretzels, melted cheese, and mustard.

As Michael got busy online, I pulled out my notebook and tried to sort my thoughts. I was a visual person, and I needed to see things spelled out. Still, it didn't matter which way I wrote things, I couldn't make sense of anything.

Why would Trina's mom say she had no idea who Rebecca was? Either she was lying or she told the truth. If she was lying then she was probably trying to cover up something. And if she told the truth . . . then Rebecca was trying to cover up something.

"Is this Rebecca?" Michael turned his screen so I could see it.

My eyes lit up. Rebecca's picture stared back at me. At least, I hadn't been imagining things when I had talked to her. I wasn't that incompetent.

"It is. What did you find out about her?"

"I found her social media profile. But there's not much information there. Only this picture and a notation that she lives in Storm River. Quite honestly, anybody could have put this together. It really means nothing."

"But at least we have a picture of her now, right?"

"It's a start." Michael turned the computer back toward him and continued to tap away on the keys.

"Could you send me that photo, just in case I need it?"

He hit a few more keys. "Done."

Just as he said the words, my phone beeped. I glanced down and saw that I had indeed gotten her picture.

As I glanced out the window at the harbor outside, I saw

a familiar face.

Was that Keith Freddie? He had said that he was getting a new job down at the docks. Maybe my investigation had just taken a turn for the better. Either he was working or he was keeping an eye on me.

I needed to talk to him.

"Excuse me for a minute," I told Michael.

"Wait, Elliot." He followed my gaze outside. "Who is that?"

"Keith Freddie, Trina's ex-boyfriend."

"I should go with you."

I glanced outside again. There were plenty of people around. "No, I'll be fine. You can keep an eye on me from the window. But I don't anticipate any problems."

I didn't stay around much longer. I was afraid I might lose Keith if I did.

Instead, I ran out the entrance of the restaurant and over toward the docks.

I froze, searching for Keith. Had I lost him already?

No, there he was. I spotted him about to climb on an oversized boat and called, "Hey, wait!"

Keith stopped in his tracks and looked at me. His eyes narrowed as if it took him a moment to recognize me.

And when he did, his narrowed gaze turned into a scowl. "What do you want? I'm trying to work. Don't get me fired."

I remembered that this man had been a suspect in my

mind at one time. His beer cans had been at that crime scene. His truck had been used to run me off the road.

Was he really innocent in all of this? I didn't know. I could only assume that the police had already talked to him.

"Did you hear about Trina?" I started.

His lips pulled down in a frown. "I did. I wasn't expecting that. I thought she had just left. Moved on to bigger and better opportunities. I've already been questioned, and obviously the police didn't arrest me. Maybe you can back off now."

I couldn't be sure, but it sounded like sincere grief in his voice.

"I'm sorry it ended this way," I said.

"And somebody stole my truck. I didn't try to run you off the road." It was like he'd anticipated what I might say next.

"That's what I heard," I said. "But that's not why I'm here to talk to you."

He glanced back at the boat as if he expected his new boss to pop out and reprimand him for socializing on the job. "And what is it? I don't have a lot of time."

"Do you have any idea who could've done this to Trina?"

He shrugged. "I wish I could tell you. After you left the other day, I ran into someone at my show. He said he heard Trina was seeing somebody else. Somebody rich."

"I know. But he has an alibi."

"What else do you want to know?" He tapped his foot.

"Anybody else you can think of who would be better off with her dead?"

He stared at a seagull that had landed on one of the pilings nearby, squawking as if it wanted to add to our conversation. Finally, Keith said, "I guess you could try her mom."

I flinched at his words. "Her mom? Why in the world would Trina's mom murder her?"

"The two had a tumultuous relationship, to say the least. I heard that she took out a life insurance policy on Trina."

Had Trina died . . . because Trina's mom might get a windfall as a result? It seemed outlandish.

I stared at him. "I don't suppose you have anything to verify that?"

"Only what Trina told me. I'm sure there's a paperwork trail somewhere. But her mom was crazy. That's part of the reason that Trina was the way she was. She had a crazy upbringing. Her mom has been married at least three times and had uncountable boyfriends in between. I heard she liked to lash out. I don't know if that was physically or emotionally but . . ."

It seemed like something worth looking into, I supposed. I remembered the bruises that people had mentioned seeing on Trina. What if there was more to that story than she let on? Could her relationship with her mom be that tumultuous?

However, if Trina's mom was guilty, then why hadn't she

had even a flash of recognition when she saw me? The killer obviously knew who I was—someone was trying to stop me from investigating.

Trina's mom didn't fit.

"Now can I go?" He started to take a step back into the boat.

"Just one more question," I said.

"Make it quick."

I pulled up Rebecca's picture on my phone. "Do you recognize this woman?"

He only looked at my phone for a moment. "Of course. It's Trina's sister, Rebecca. Why?"

So Trina had told him that Rebecca was her sister.

Maybe Rebecca wasn't the crazy one after all. Maybe it was Trina's mom. And maybe Rebecca was doing the smart thing by keeping her distance from her.

Could I add Trina's mom to my suspect list? I supposed nothing was off the table at this point. Maybe the woman was just a great actress and had pretended not to recognize me.

But I didn't want to believe that was true. However, as Michael said, we needed to follow the evidence.

Did Hunter know about this life insurance policy? Should I call and let him know?

As I stepped back toward the restaurant, my phone buzzed.

Surprise washed through me when I saw a photo pop up on my screen.

A photo of Stacy. A gag was over her mouth, and tears glistened in her eyes.

Under the image of her fear-filled face were the words:

Come to 581 Sandstone Court. Come alone. You have fifteen minutes. Tell anyone, and Stacy will die.

I sucked in a breath. Was this really happening right now?

I stared at the photo again.

Yes, it was.

What should I do?

I glanced up at the restaurant. I was just out of sight from Michael right now. If I walked fast enough, I could get into my car and drive away before he could stop me.

But I wasn't sure that would be the smartest thing to do.

CHAPTER THIRTY

I PULLED up to a house on the other side of town. I had to buy some time until backup arrived. I had no other choice.

Not if I wanted Stacy to live.

As I sat there, my phone buzzed again.

My hands were sweating as I gripped the device and read the words there.

Leave your phone and your purse in the car. I hope you came alone, because if you didn't, Stacy will die.

I could hardly breathe. I shouldn't be here. Yet how could I not be here? I had to help Stacy if I could. I didn't want to find another dead body, like I had found Trina.

But I also had to be smart. After grabbing something from my purse, I did as the caller asked. I left my things in the car and walked toward the house. The place was in an area where I'd never been. It was the wrong side of the wrong side of the tracks, if that made sense.

The windows on the bungalow had been boarded up, the concrete steps were busted, and the yard overgrown with weeds.

Did someone actually live here?

There was no car in the driveway, and I couldn't see into the back of the house.

But with every step I took, my nerves doubled.

This was a bad, bad idea—especially as I remembered being in that dark warehouse last night and discovering Trina's body.

I tried the front door. It was unlocked.

My throat burned as I stepped inside the dark place and looked around. "Hello?"

There was no answer.

I kept walking. Kept listening. Kept waiting for a clue as to what was going to happen next.

I walked through the living room. The kitchen. Down the hallway toward the bedrooms.

The deeper I walked down the hallway, the more the darkness around me grew. The boarded-up windows didn't let any light in.

Would I come out of this alive?

I wasn't sure. I could only hope.

I heard a footstep behind me and froze.

"You came alone," a voice said. "Just like I asked. Good job."

I slowly turned, instantly recognizing the female voice.

I knew exactly who was behind this crime.

As I'd driven over here, a theory had formed in my mind. A mental image that I didn't want to believe was true.

But it was.

I knew it.

A light came on, and illumination filled the space.

Someone shoved me into the room to my left. As I stumbled inside, I spotted Stacy sitting against the wall, tied to a chair, with a gag over her mouth.

My gaze went back to the killer.

A woman with red eyes, a gun in her trembling hands, and a look in her gaze that showed reality was located in a distant galaxy. There was more than that—there was also desperation and fear.

I was going to have to proceed very carefully, or Stacy and I were going to end up dead.

Even though the text said I needed to come alone or Stacy would die, I knew the only reason someone would want me to come was so this person could hurt—and silence—me.

"Rebecca," I said. "I'm here. You can let Stacy go."

"You weren't supposed to figure this out," Rebecca said through gritted teeth.

"Then why did you hire me?"

"I set up that other evidence." Spittle flew from her mouth as each of her words came out with an exaggerated bark. "You were supposed to go where it led. It wasn't supposed to come back to me."

"So you left those beer cans at the scene? You knew they would lead back to Keith. And that's why you stole his truck also, isn't it?"

"Everything was in place." Her voice quivered. "I'm not sure why you're still looking for the killer when it's obvious who he is."

I glanced at Stacy again. Her wide eyes stared at me, begging for help.

I tried to silently reassure her, but I wasn't sure if my gaze communicated that or not.

Instead, I swallowed hard as I looked back at Rebecca. "Trina's mom said Trina doesn't have a sister."

Rebecca sneered. "Trina's mom is an idiot. She always said Trina was going to end up getting herself killed. That's probably why she got that life insurance policy. Trina told me all about it."

"You mean, she really did get that policy?"

"Yes. Mrs. Morrison was my second fall guy, in case all of this fell through." She pointed her gun at Stacy, a deep, bitter frown pulling at her lips.

"So are you Trina's sister or not?" I asked, buying time.

"I am. Our dad got a woman pregnant, and I was born. It's not officially on record that Trina and I are related, but we are. We only discovered each other about three years ago."

"Trina's mom didn't know about you?" What sense did that make?

"Probably not." Rebecca snorted. "She's so deep into the drug culture that all her brain cells are dying. She doesn't care about anyone but herself. It's probably where Trina got it."

I shook my head, still trying to put all the pieces together as I stared at Rebecca's gun. "I thought you loved Trina. Why would you kill her?"

She let out a skeptical chuckle. "You thought you had things figured out, but you didn't. When I told you to let this go, you should have. You were never supposed to come this close to the truth."

"You slashed my tires, didn't you? And tried to run me off the road?"

"I realized that hiring you was a mistake. I had to figure out a way to get you off the case without being too obvious."

I needed to try a different tactic. "I know that Trina tried to leave you, just like she's left everybody else."

Rebecca's face darkened.

"You've been on the verge of losing it for a while," I continued. "But when she met someone new and looked so happy without you, that put you over the edge."

She said nothing.

"But I still can't figure out why you killed her. Was it

because she hit you? Did you guys get into some type of fist-fight and this was all an accident?"

Her chuckle deepened. "Is that what you think? No, it wasn't like that. She did hit me—but only after I hit her first."

I sucked in a breath as a more complete picture formed in my mind. "Why would you hit your sister?"

"She wouldn't listen to anybody. I was trying to talk some sense into her. But we ended up getting into a fight." Rebecca touched the scarred side of her face. "Trina was trying to hold me back when this happened."

"So Trina was trying to help you?" Had I really gotten things so mixed up?

"We made up afterward. But then I saw how stupid she was being. She wouldn't listen to anybody."

"So you followed her to McCaverty's, didn't you? You knew that she wanted to fix that place up. And you tried to talk some more sense into her, didn't you?"

"I did," she sneered. "But she wouldn't listen to me."

"What happened next?" I asked, stepping closer to Stacy.

"That's when I knew I had to stop her, for good. But I didn't mean to kill her. I didn't think I had hit her that hard. But I did." Her voice cracked, and moisture filled her eyes.

"So you accidentally killed your sister. Okay. But why hire me to find the killer?" I needed to kill more time before Rebecca truly became desperate and did something irreversible.

Her hand flew through the air, and her eyes grew wider.

"Because I'm going crazy. I can't sleep at night. I just keep waiting for the police to come and arrest me."

"You could have turned yourself in."

"I don't want my life to be spent in jail. That's where my dad is now. I don't want to be like him. That's why I planted evidence—so that somebody else would be arrested and maybe I could actually sleep at night if I didn't think I'd be found out."

I nodded at Stacy and her wide, scared eyes. "But you grabbed Stacy instead?"

Rebecca wasn't making any sense. How did Stacy fit into all of this? Besides, it wasn't a cold-blooded murder, Trina had died in the heat of the moment.

It didn't make Rebecca innocent, but it didn't make her someone who planned to hurt other people either.

However, this moment of desperation might disprove all of that.

"I realized you were getting too close to the truth," Rebecca said. "I tried to tell you to back off, but you wouldn't do it. My warnings to you went unheeded, so I had to come up with a backup plan. I called Stacy, pretending to be Trina, and asked her to meet me at McCaverty's."

"What happened then?" I tried to picture it all happening in my head.

Rebecca's sneer turned toward Stacy. "She met me. I was going to make it look like she'd killed Trina. It made sense, right? Especially since all the evidence I planted to implicate Keith wasn't working out. But then you showed up."

"Stacy was the one who screamed last night?"

"That's right. You showing up there really ruined my plans. I subdued Stacy, and then I had to knock you out before the police got there. I didn't think I was going to get away in time."

"I didn't see any other cars there."

"I parked on the other side. You didn't make it that far."

"This still seems really extreme, Rebecca. Maybe your guilt would go away if you'd just turn yourself in."

"Trina just wouldn't listen to anyone!" Rebecca's voice climbed. She was in no mood to listen to logic. Her emotions were still screaming too loud. "She was making bad choices. And I knew she was going to disappear from my life just like she always did. But she was all I had. My mom is dead. My dad is in jail. I only had Trina. And she didn't care."

"That had to be hard." I meant the words. None of that justified murder, of course.

Her eyes narrowed. "I was done with Trina. I just wanted to talk some sense into her. But things turned ugly."

"You don't have to bring Stacy into this." I moved until I stood in front of Stacy, my body blocking hers.

"I need a scapegoat."

"What are you thinking, Rebecca?" I almost didn't want to know the answer to that question. What I needed was to figure a way out of this situation.

If I made a run for it, Rebecca would just kill Stacy. I couldn't let that happen. My only other option was to take Rebecca out. Although I had some self-defense classes under my belt, Rebecca had a gun right now.

I didn't.

"You guys have left me no choice but to kill you both." Rebecca raised her gun toward me, and I sucked in a breath, waiting to feel a bullet pierce my flesh.

CHAPTER THIRTY-ONE

IF I WAS GOING to do something, I had to do it soon.

With my body angled away from Rebecca, I reached into my back pocket. There was only one weapon I had right now at my disposal.

And I wasn't sure that my plan would work.

"You don't want to do this," I told Rebecca, giving one last ditch effort that I might talk some sense into her.

"I don't want to go to jail for this." She shook her head, her eyes wide and crazy.

"You don't think you're going to get caught?" She was smarter than that, right? She had to know there was no happy ending here.

"I still have a plan. I can make it look like Stacy killed you and then herself. I texted you from her phone, after all. If that doesn't work, I can make it look like Keith did this."

Sweat formed on her face. "It's not too late to plant more evidence, maybe leave a flyer here for one of his awful cover band concerts. I can come up with some kind of cover story."

"Keith is at work right now. People have seen him there. They're going to know he's not responsible."

She nudged her gun out even farther. "Shut up! I'm going to figure this out, one way or another."

Her finger hooked around the trigger as if she was preparing to shoot me.

I sucked in a breath. Where was my backup? They should be here by now.

I heard another footstep.

As Rebecca turned toward the sound, I pulled out the objects in my pocket and tossed them at her face.

She screamed with pain.

My mom's sewing pins.

I knew they would come in handy one day. I'd grabbed them from my purse and put them in my pocket before I'd come in.

As she grabbed her face, a figure dove from the hallway and tackled her.

While Hunter pinned Rebecca's arms behind her back, I grabbed the gun, making sure to keep it out of her reach.

Of course, I hadn't come here without telling anybody. That was rule number one when it came to saving someone's life. Never go alone, no matter what the bad guy wanted you to do.

Speaking of which . . .

Michael rushed into the room, two officers behind him. As he did, Hunter began to read Rebecca her rights.

"You good?" Michael asked.

I nodded. "I am."

Without wasting any more time, I rushed toward Stacy and pulled the gag from her mouth.

"Thank you." Her voice sounded hoarse with emotion.

"Of course." I tried to work the ropes at her hands, but they were tied too tight. I would need someone with a knife to help me. "I'm sorry you got pulled into this."

"I should have known better than to meet her at McCaverty's. But I thought it was Trina. I really did."

"Rebecca fooled a lot of people. Don't beat yourself up."

Her eyes softened. "I thought I was going to die."

As two officers led Rebecca away and another detective went to help Stacy, Hunter approached me. Michael stood by my side, almost like he was my personal bodyguard.

"Good work, Elliot," Hunter said, his eyes a mix of unapproving and impressed.

"Thanks." I felt like I should feel more victorious, but I didn't. "I can't believe Rebecca tricked me like she did. How could I have believed her so easily?"

Michael offered a compassionate smile. "It happens to the best of us."

Was that true? Or was he just trying to make me feel better?

I didn't know. But I was happy that Stacy had gotten a happy ending, at least.

"Turns out that Rebecca has been living here," Hunter said. "Her dad used to own this place, but it's been condemned for a while now. I guess she had nowhere else to go when he went to jail. She was too old for foster care, so she came here."

"That's . . . sad."

"Her real last name is Walters," Hunter continued. "She's in the process of changing it to Morrison. Maybe she wanted to feel like she had a family again."

"Even sadder," I muttered.

But, that said, it didn't matter what a person had been through. Whatever those heartaches were, they didn't justify hurting other people.

The good news was that I'd solved this case—though barely.

The other good news was that I'd lived to tell about it.

I'd consider that a win.

CHAPTER THIRTY-TWO

MICHAEL STOPPED by my house the next day after Chloe's soccer game. The girl was glowing beside her father, kicking a soccer ball up on her knees as we stood in the front yard.

"How was your game?" I asked, leaning down to eye level.

"It was great." She grinned, her lips lined with what looked like red fruit punch.

"Did you win?"

"Nope. But my dad said as long as I give it my best, I'm doing okay."

I raised my hand and gave her a high five. "My dad used to always say that the best way you could win was by having a good attitude."

She grabbed my arm. "The floor is lava!"

She jumped onto an old paver stone at the edge of the

flowerbed. Further adding to the confusion, Michael jumped onto the front step.

"The floor is lava?" I questioned. What in the world were these people doing?

"It's a game," Chloe explained. "You have to find something to stand on or your feet will burn off."

"Oh . . ." I quickly found an oversized rock in the flowerbed and stood there, trying precariously to balance myself. "Does this work?"

"For now! Don't fall off or you're going to die!"

"I can't have that happen . . ."

Michael glanced at me and smiled.

Just as quickly as the game had started, Chloe hopped down and began kicking her ball across the yard. That attention span seemed about right for a seven-year-old.

I turned to Michael. "What brings you guys by?"

"Oscar called me this morning, and he wants to offer you your job back," Michael said, hands in his pockets.

"Why didn't Oscar tell me about it himself?" Wouldn't that make more sense?

"Because why would Oscar do something himself when he could have his paid staff do it for him?"

I couldn't even argue Michael's point. *That* seemed totally like Oscar.

"I'm going to need to come to an understanding with Oscar," I finally said. "He can't fire me every week."

"He can. And he might. But it's your choice. You don't have to keep working for him."

"Noted." I'd come to realize that my meddling this week had felt a little more like peddling—peddling lies and deceit. I didn't like that. Yet I loved finding answers.

How could I find a balance between the two?

I'd also remembered that trip my dad took me on to see the migrating dorado catfish. Sometimes, to get the results you wanted, it took time and effort. And sometimes it felt like those answers would never come, that you were wasting time.

But when the payout happened, it was worth it.

I had to remember that now also.

Good things did come to those who waited.

Michael studied me for a minute. "So what are you going to tell Oscar?"

"I'll think about it." But I already knew the answer. I was going to go back and work for the man. I still had a lot to learn—especially if I wanted to find my father's killer.

Michael glanced back at Chloe, who started to wander back toward us. "Go kick the ball in the grass for a minute, okay, sweetie?"

Chloe didn't argue. She happily began doing drills as she drifted away.

As Michael turned toward me and stuffed his hands more deeply into his pockets, I knew that whatever he was about to say was something he felt strongly about.

"I have a confession," he started. "I was the one who told Oscar you had taken Rebecca's case on the side."

My eyes widened at his words. "Why would you do that?"

"I didn't want to see you get hurt. I had a feeling this case was going to be ugly, and I knew you were wrapped up in it. I thought that might discourage you from continuing. But it didn't. I didn't actually think he was going to fire you on the spot, though."

"Why couldn't you have just told me that?"

He shrugged again. "I should have. And I'm sorry. I've been all out of sorts this week."

I let my heart fall to the side as I studied him. "What's going on?"

"I've been trying to figure out this single parenting thing. You would think after seven years that I would have mastered it, right? But Chloe has a mother/daughter event coming up in a couple weeks. You know, Mother's Day? She's been pretty upset since she doesn't have anybody to go with her. I usually try to brush these things off, to make them seem like they're not a big deal. But I'm having trouble doing that this year."

"Can't your mother attend with her?"

"She's going out of town that week. She tried to rearrange her schedule, but it didn't work."

"I'm sorry," I said. "I'm sure you'll figure something out."

He nodded. "I'm sure I will. But despite my bad mood, I shouldn't have handled the situation the way that I did. I just wanted to say I'm sorry."

"You're forgiven," I said. "You've gotten me out of some tough situations, so maybe we're even now."

He offered a smile. "Thanks, Elliot. You're a good sport. That's a true fact."

As he opened his mouth to say more, a truck pulled in front of my house.

I knew exactly who that was.

But Michael's eyes narrowed as he stared at the person who stepped out.

"I'm here to give you an estimate on some new decking." The man stopped in his tracks when he spotted Michael and me.

Part of me thought he might dart away. But instead he hung his head and his shoulders slumped with defeat.

Nolan Burke.

"Okay, okay," he muttered. "You caught me. I guess you really don't want a deck to be built?"

I shook my head. "No, I don't."

"Then I've got nothing else to say here." With his tail still between his legs, Burke walked back to his truck.

Michael turned to me and gave me a questioning look. "What . . . ? How . . . ?"

"While I was waiting for Frank Stephens to come out of his office, I bought a newspaper to cover my face with. I was reading the classifieds, and I saw somebody had advertised themselves as a low-cost deck builder. There was something about the words that had me curious. It was called Eden

Lane Decking. Eden Lane was where Burke lived. So I called the number."

"And Nolan Burke showed up here," Michael finished. "But we already did everything we needed to do on that case. Why did you keep pushing it?"

"Because I wanted to know the truth. I wanted to know if Nolan Burke was really helping his grandmother build a deck or not. It turns out, he is a fraud. He started to collect the insurance money and to make money on the side. I'll sleep better at night knowing that."

Michael let out a chuckle. "You are one of a kind, Elliot Ransom."

"Maybe I am," I said. "But my dad always said originals were the best."

"And your dad had it right."

COMING NEXT: THE EXERCISE OF INTERFERING

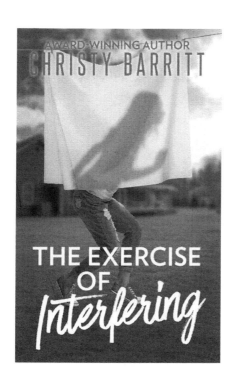

ALSO BY CHRISTY BARRITT:

YOU MIGHT ALSO ENJOY ...

THE SQUEAKY CLEAN MYSTERY SERIES

On her way to completing a degree in forensic science, Gabby St. Claire drops out of school and starts her own crime-scene cleaning business. When a routine cleaning job uncovers a murder weapon the police overlooked, she realizes that the wrong person is in jail. She also realizes that crime scene cleaning might be the perfect career for utilizing her investigative skills.

THE WORST DETECTIVE EVER:

I'm not really a private detective. I just play one on TV.

Joey Darling, better known to the world as Raven Remington, detective extraordinaire, is trying to separate herself from her invincible alter ego. She played the spunky character for five years on the hit TV show *Relentless*, which catapulted her to fame and into the role of Hollywood's sweetheart. When her marriage falls apart, her finances dwindle to nothing, and her father disappears, Joey finds herself on the Outer Banks of North Carolina, trying to piece together her life away from the limelight. But as people continually mistake her for the character she played on TV, she's tasked with solving real life crimes ... even though she's terrible at it.

ABOUT THE AUTHOR

USA Today has called Christy Barritt's books "scary, funny, passionate, and quirky."

Christy writes both mystery and romantic suspense novels that are clean with underlying messages of faith. Her books have won the Daphne du Maurier Award for Excellence in Suspense and Mystery, have been twice nominated for the Romantic Times Reviewers' Choice Award, and have finaled for both a Carol Award and Foreword Magazine's Book of the Year.

She is married to her Prince Charming, a man who thinks she's hilarious—but only when she's not trying to be. Christy is a self-proclaimed klutz, an avid music lover who's known for spontaneously bursting into song, and a road trip aficionado.

When she's not working or spending time with her family, she enjoys singing, playing the guitar, and exploring small, unsuspecting towns where people have no idea how accident-prone she is.

Find Christy online at:
    www.christybarritt.com
    www.facebook.com/christybarritt
    www.twitter.com/cbarritt

Sign up for Christy's newsletter to get information on all of her latest releases here: **www.christybarritt.com/newsletter-sign-up/**

If you enjoyed this book, please consider leaving a review.